After lunch, given by the local Girl Scouts, the mayor suddenly said, "Well, I'm afraid I'll have to leave you two on your own for the rest of the day. Centennial Week is all well and good, but I've still got a city government to run. I'm sure you'll both do fine."

"At last, we're alone!" Jeff, the Centennial Week King said. He leaned back against the plush blue velour of the limousine and casually draped his arm around Susan's shoulders.

She stiffened. What on earth did Jeff think he was doing? Then she remembered that he thought it was *Chris* he was with. Oh, dear, she thought. Chris never mentioned anything about her and Jeff being interested in each other! How would she, Susan, get out of this gracefully, without ruining things for her sister?

Susan thought fast. Then, in her most teasing Chris-voice, she said, "Now, Jeffrey Miller, I think you're forgetting that you're a public figure. Honestly," she went on in mock horror, "have you ever seen Prince Charles and Lady Di carry on in public?"

Another Juniper Book
by Cynthia Blair

THE BANANA SPLIT AFFAIR

THE HOT FUDGE SUNDAY AFFAIR

Cynthia Blair

FAWCETT JUNIPER • NEW YORK

RLI: $\dfrac{\text{VL: Grade 5 + up}}{\text{IL: Grade 6 + up}}$

A Fawcett Juniper Book
Published by Ballantine Books

Library of Congress Catalog Card Number: 85-91258

ISBN: 0-449-70158-1

Manufactured in the United States of America

First Edition: November 1985

One

"*I'm so* bored!" *wailed Christine Pratt. Dramat-*ically, she flopped back against the green canvas hammock that was hung between the two largest oak trees in her family's backyard. "I've been counting the weeks until summer vacation, and now that it's here, I don't know *what* I'm going to do with myself for the next two months!"

Susan, her twin sister, looked up from the patch of string beans and tomatoes she was weeding. "Well, for one thing, we promised Mom we'd get this garden in shape. I don't know about you, but I enjoy working outside. Besides, it's rewarding, knowing that by the end of the summer we'll have lots of fresh vegetables that we grew all by ourselves."

"Oh, Sooz, you're always so *practical*! That's not what I mean. I'm talking about something fun, something adventurous . . . something different! I want to meet new people, see new places, do new things." Chris let her arm drop over the side of the

1

hammock. Lazily she picked a dandelion out of the lawn. "Instead, I'll probably just sit around the house, doing nothing."

"You make it sound like you've been sentenced to two months of solitary confinement!" Susan couldn't help chuckling as she plopped down on the ground cross-legged, glad for the chance to take a break. As always, her sister was being melodramatic. The truth was that the popular Chris Pratt would no doubt be busy night and day, running off to the town pool and parties and barbecues and Fozzy's, the brand-new ice cream parlor in town. Her large group of friends was always planning something, and they weren't about to leave Chris behind.

"What about you, Sooz? What have you got lined up? Besides digging in the dirt and taking advantage of that green thumb of yours, I mean."

"Oh, you know me. I'm anxious to start fooling around with that new set of watercolors I just got and do some experimenting with pastels. And I've already got a huge stack of books that I can't wait to read." She shrugged. "Actually, I'm looking forward to having some time to myself."

Although the two sixteen-year-olds were identical twins, there was little that Susan and Christine Pratt had in common. Chris was talkative and outgoing, traits that made her one of the most popular girls at Whittington High. Her life seemed to be a whirlwind of club meetings, outings with girlfriends, and dates. In fact, the rest of the family had practically stopped answering the telephone, since it was almost always someone calling for Chris.

Susan, on the other hand, was quiet. Not only was she naturally shy; she preferred being on her own, pursuing the hobbies that were important to her. Reading and listening to music were favorite pastimes, but painting was her true passion. Her artistic talent and her self-discipline to work on developing it had already won her recognition. The year before, the school principal had chosen a painting of hers from dozens of others to put up in his office.

The girls even managed to look different. It was true that they shared the same dark brown eyes, high cheekbones, and pert ski-jump noses. But today, for example, they hardly looked alike at all. Susan's shoulder-length chestnut hair was tucked underneath a bright red bandana, while Chris's was pulled back into a flattering ponytail. Susan had donned an old pair of jeans and a navy-blue tee-shirt, printed with WHITTINGTON HIGH in yellow across the front. Chris, meanwhile, looked almost like a fashion model, decked out in khaki-colored shorts and a lavender tee-shirt that showed off her tall slim frame. The differences in their personalities were clearly reflected in their appearances.

"Besides," Susan continued, twirling a piece of grass between two fingers, "you and I deserve a rest. We worked hard in school this year. It'll be nice to relax for a change!"

"I suppose. I guess we do deserve a rest." Chris sighed. "You know, I still can't believe I got an A in history. Especially since it used to be my worst subject. And I owe that A entirely to you!"

"Well, I wouldn't say *that*, exactly. . . ."

"Come on, don't be so modest! You know darn well that if you hadn't helped me, I never would have been able to write that super research paper on the history of our town! You told me where to find things in the library and came up with the idea of checking public records over at City Hall. . . . You even wrote the outline for me!"

"I guess I did help a little."

"You sure did. And not only did I get an A; Mr. Simpson thought the project was so good that he sent a copy to the mayor. Now *that's* what I call team effort!"

"That reminds me: We have the town's one-hundred-year anniversary to look forward to this July," said Susan. "Imagine: Whittington's been around for a whole century. And I hear they're planning all kinds of things for the celebration. Parades, picnics, speeches—and the dedication of that new statue, or whatever it is. Centennial Week should be the biggest thing that's happened in this town since they built the pool!"

"Yes, I guess that'll be fun," Chris admitted. But her sullenness continued as she picked apart the dandelion petal by petal.

Before the exasperated Susan could say anything else, she noticed her mother coming toward them, carrying a tray with three tall icy glasses.

"Hi, girls!" Mrs. Pratt called. "I can see you're working hard!" As she got nearer, she said, "I brought out some lemonade because I figured you'd be due for a break around now. I can see I was right!"

"We've been working like positive *fiends* all morning." Gratefully, Chris took one of the glasses off the tray and gulped down half the lemonade without stopping. "Working in the sun really dries you out."

"So I see!" Mrs. Pratt handed a glass to Susan, then joined Chris on the hammock. "You girls have gotten a lot done. I'm very impressed!"

"If you're impressed now," said Susan, looking at the neat patch she'd been working on for the past hour, "wait until you see the huge tomatoes we have in August."

"At the rate you're going, we'll have to set up a stand in front of the house just to get rid of them all!"

Chris had already downed the rest of her lemonade. "Hey," she suddenly asked, "what's that in your pocket?"

"Oh, just this morning's mail. I haven't even looked at it." She took a small stack of envelopes out of the front pocket of her skirt and glanced through it. "Nothing too interesting, I'm afraid. Just the usual advertisements, a couple of bills . . . why, here's one for you, Chris."

"For me? I'm not expecting anything." Excitedly, she reached for the white envelope. It looked very formal, typed with her address and full name: Ms. Christine Pratt. And the address on the upper left corner was Mayor Harris, City Hall of Whittington. "It's from the mayor!" she cried, tearing open the envelope.

"Uh-oh," joked her twin. "Guess they finally caught you, Sis. Now you're in for it."

Chris ignored her. She was too busy reading the letter.

"For heaven's sake, *tell* us!" her mother pleaded

after a few seconds. "Can't you see we're both dying to know why the mayor is writing to you?"

Suddenly Chris started screeching. "I don't believe it! I don't believe it!" She was beside herself with glee. "What'll I wear? Oh, no; I'd better get my hair cut right away. . . . Oh, I don't believe it!"

"Chris, what on earth are you talking about?" Susan had joined her mother and sister on the hammock. Impatiently, she snatched the letter from her hand and began to read out loud.

"Dear Ms. Pratt:
"As you probably know, Whittington is celebrating its one hundredth anniversary this year. We have been busily planning a week of festivities for July, called Centennial Week. To better include our citizens in the celebration, we have decided to select an honorary King and Queen from the local high school. After reading your most informative research project on the town's history, we have chosen you to be our Queen."

"Chris, that's fantastic! Congratulations!"

"My own daughter, queen of Whittington!" Mrs. Pratt was almost as excited as Chris.

"I bet you'll get your picture on the front page of the *Whittington Herald*!" Susan exclaimed.

"And you'll be at the dedication ceremony for the new monument."

"And maybe you'll even get to read your research project or at least get it printed in the newspaper!"

Suddenly Chris grew serious. In fact, she was frowning so deeply that she looked as if she were about to cry.

"Chris, what is it?" Her twin was concerned. "Is everything all right?"

"Well . . . I just realized something."

"What?"

"That *you* did just as much work on that research paper as *I* did. Yet I'm the one who's getting all the glory. And the fun of being queen of Centennial Week."

"That's very fair of you," her mother said gently. "But I don't see what can be done about it. After all, there can be only one queen, and you're the one who was selected. You're the one the mayor wants."

She stood up, gathering together the rest of the mail. "Cheer up, Chris. I'm sure Susan doesn't mind, do you, honey? Now, if you'll excuse me, I'm going to telephone everyone I know and spread the good news. Goodness, if you're the queen, I guess that makes me the Queen Mother, doesn't it?" She hurried off, beaming with pride.

But the scene she left behind was a somber one. Now that her sister had pointed out that she had played a large part in the success of the research project that was responsible for Chris's being awarded this honor, Susan, too, was pensive. The two girls sat in silence for a long time. Finally Susan spoke.

"Mom's right, you know. You *were* the one chosen."

"I know. It's just that I won't feel nearly as good

about it, knowing that you're at home or watching from the sidelines.''

"Don't worry," Susan insisted bravely. "Look, Chris, you've just been awarded a great honor! And it's going to be a blast! You should be *happy* about it, not worried about how I'll feel. I'm glad for you."

"You don't mind?"

"Not at all."

"You're sure you don't feel bad, Sooz?"

"No. I *promise*."

"Well . . . okay, then. Let's get back to work." Chris climbed out of the hammock, picked up a trowel, and with new enthusiasm attacked a patch of dandelions. Without realizing it, she had started to hum.

Susan, meanwhile, bent over a row of string bean seedlings and began weeding furiously. She wanted to make sure that her sister didn't see that there were tears in her eyes.

Two

For the next two weeks Chris's life centered around getting ready for her upcoming reign as the honorary queen of Whittington's Centennial Week. It seemed as if there was so much to do. Mainly she wanted to review her research on the town's history. After all, she reasoned, she *was* supposed to be an expert of sorts. Beyond that she needed to get her hair cut, have her good shoes reheeled, and decide what to wear to each event. Her mother agreed that a new dress or two was definitely in order for such a special occasion, and she looked forward to a shopping spree.

Susan was as helpful as she could be. She was determined not to put a damper on her twin's growing excitement. In fact, she became so wrapped up in plans and speculations about the approaching week of festivities that she almost forgot about her initial resentment. She seemed to be enjoying the preparations almost as much as her sister. Still, she was a bit surprised that Chris didn't mention the issue of fairness again.

Chris hadn't forgotten, however. Knowing that she was about to embark on an adventure that her twin rightfully deserved to share nagged at her constantly, hanging over her like a little gray cloud. But she decided not to say any more about it. At least not yet.

When the beginning of Centennial Week was just three days away, the girls went off to the local shopping mall together, gleeful about their mission of finding just the right dress. After considering every single one in the entire mall, Chris and Susan finally found some possibilities on the fourth floor of one of its department stores. Upon her sister's insistence, Susan followed her into the dressing room to provide assistance with buttons and zippers—and advice.

"What do you think of this one, Sooz?" Chris surveyed herself in the full-length mirror, first striking a modellike pose, then frowning and placing her hands on her hips. "Too severe, don't you think?"

Susan examined the simple navy-blue dress with the white lace collar. "Definitely not you," she agreed. "It doesn't exactly capture the spirit of Centennial Week, either."

Chris tried the second. It was obvious that she had her doubts about this light blue flowered sundress, too. She stood before the mirror, scowling. "Too casual?"

"I don't know; I kind of like it." Susan played around with the scarf that came with it, draping it around Chris's neck and shoulders so that it hung in soft, flattering folds. "How about if you wore it like that?"

"Oh, you're right! It's gorgeous! And just right for a really hot day. Something like a picnic or maybe a parade." Chris still wasn't entirely convinced, but she trusted her sister's judgment. Especially in the area of what kinds of clothes were suitable for someone about to become a public figure.

The third dress was instantly deemed perfect by Susan. It was dressier, just the thing for a dinner or some other formal occasion. The lines were simple. What made it distinctive was the way it fit, the soft texture of the fabric, and the colors, a subtle design of rosy pinks and pale lavenders.

Her eyes glowed as she fondled the fabric. "It's beautiful, Chris." Her voice was filled with longing. "I definitely think you should get this one."

Suddenly Chris began pulling it off. "Okay, I'll take it. But here, why don't you try it on first?"

"Chris, whatever for?"

Chris shrugged. "I'm curious to see how it looks on somebody else. Besides," she added with a laugh, "since you and I look alike, it's a good way for me to know how *I* look in it."

Susan obediently put on the pink-and-lavender dress. It was no surprise that she looked just like her twin sister in it. What did surprise her, however, was how special it made her feel. That delicate puff of a dress, with its silky fabric and luscious pastel colors, made her feel . . . well, like a queen.

The next stop was the beauty parlor, down at the other end of the mall. Susan had planned to wait while Chris got a haircut. She'd even brought along a book to keep herself busy. But when they reached Danielle's Hair Boutique, there was a big sign in the window, announcing a summer sale.

"Oh, look!" Chris cried, grabbing her sister's arm. "There's a special on haircuts today! Only half their usual price. Why don't you get your hair cut, too?"

"Do you think I need it?" Susan automatically reached up to touch her own chestnut hair. She realized that she was due for a trim. It was hanging just below her shoulders.

"Why not? With this sale, we've got enough money. Come on, it'll be good for you!" Bodily she dragged her twin inside the shop.

An hour later, they emerged together, with their hair freshly washed, cut, and blow-dried. As they passed a mirror in the window of a housewares store, Susan stopped. "Hey, look, Chris. Right now you and I look more alike than ever!" It was true; since their hair had been cut by the same person, in the exact same way, it was virtually impossible to tell them apart.

That evening, at home, Chris was anxious to show off her new purchases. "Let's try everything on and show Mom and Dad how we look."

"How *we* look? They're your clothes, Chris!"

"I know. But instead of me trying them on one at a time, let's each put one of the dresses on. It'll be fun. And you can wear the pink one."

"Well . . . okay. But I think you're acting kind of strange, Christine Pratt!"

Chris just smiled mysteriously.

Their parents were in the backyard, getting ready for a family barbecue. Their mother was lighting the coals while their father traipsed back and forth from the kitchen, bringing paper plates and silverware and lemonade out to the picnic table on the lawn.

"What's this?" Mrs. Pratt asked, looking up from the grill. "A fashion show?"

"In a way. These are the two dresses I got today for Centennial Week. What do you think?" Chris and Susan twirled around, showing off their brandnew finery. "This one's for daytime," Chris explained. "And the one Susan is wearing is for more formal events. You know, like parties and dinners."

"You both look lovely."

"Your mother's right; you do look terrific," Mr. Pratt said approvingly. "In fact, I'd say that either one of you could easily be the queen of Centennial Week. I'd be hard-pressed to choose one of you over the other. You both look worthy of the honor. And I'm speaking as one of Whittington's oldest, most distinguished citizens." His eyes twinkled. "Well, oldest, anyway."

"Oh, Daddy!" Chris laughed. "We'd better get ready for dinner. Come on, Sooz. Let's go upstairs and change."

While Susan was putting on jeans and a tee-shirt, her sister came into her room. She stood there in silence for a minute, staring at the paintings on the wall, all of them done by Susan. But Susan had the feeling that it wasn't her artwork her twin was thinking about.

"You know," Chris said slowly, "I've been

giving this a lot of thought. The unfairness of me being picked as queen of Centennial Week, I mean, even though you deserve it as much as I do."

"I thought we'd already decided that you weren't going to worry about that anymore."

"I know. But I keep thinking of something Mom said. She said, 'There can be only one queen.'"

"Well, she's right."

"And then what Daddy just said. About both of us looking as if we're 'worthy of the honor.' And that he'd be hard-pressed to choose one of us over the other."

"Yes, but I'm afraid I still don't follow."

"Sooz, remember when you and I traded lives for two weeks? When we pretended to be each other so we could see what each other's lives were like?"

"Of course. You mean the Banana Split Affair."

That had been the twins' code name for their scheme of switching identities to see what it was like to be the other. They had chosen that name because Susan had bet Chris that it wouldn't work—and the stakes were a banana split at the end of the two weeks.

But it *had* worked. They managed to convince everyone that Chris was Susan and Susan was Chris. Even their parents couldn't tell them apart.

Susan glanced over at her sister. "Why do I have a sneaking suspicion that you're cooking up something similar?"

"Listen. Last time you and I pretended we were each other, right? And we were great at it! This time how about if you and I pretend to be the *same* person?"

"The same person?"

"Right. We can both take turns being Christine Pratt!"

"I don't know, Chris. . . ."

"But the mayor doesn't know me! Most of the people that the queen of Centennial Week will be meeting don't know me, either! And they certainly won't know that I have a twin sister!"

"So you're saying that one day you'd be queen and the next day I'd show up, pretending to be you, and *I'd* get to be queen."

"Exactly. That way we'd both get to go to some of the dinners and some of the parties and some of the parades. . . . We'd share the fun!"

"Just like we shared the work that got you this chance in the first place." Susan was beginning to come around. "You know, I think you're right. Maybe it could work."

"Of course it could! Let's do it! *Please!* Otherwise it won't be any fun for me. Not when I know you're home or watching from the sidelines."

Slowly a grin crept over Susan's face. "Well, I've got nothing to lose. Yes, I'm game!"

"Terrific!" Chris reached over and gave her sister a big hug.

"Hey, I just realized something, you little sneak." Susan's eyes narrowed. "You've been planning this all along, haven't you? That's why you insisted that I get my hair cut at the same time you did. And that's why you made me try on that pink dress. I wouldn't be surprised if the reason you *bought* that dress is that I liked it so much!"

"Guilty, I'm afraid."

"You little devil! And you never let on!"

"Well," Chris said with a shrug, "you can't blame me for waiting for just the right time, can you?"

Suddenly she grew more serious. "Hey, Sooz, there's only one thing."

"What?"

"Last time around, we told Mom and Dad about our plan, remember?"

"Yes . . ."

"This time let's not tell anybody."

Susan was doubtful. "Are you sure? What about . . . ? What if . . . ?"

"Look. In the first place, they'd never let us do it, even though the whole thing is perfectly harmless. I think Mom and Dad would be afraid we'd get caught—which of course we both know will never happen. And in the second place, well, I just think it'll be a lot more fun this way!"

"Well . . . okay," Susan agreed reluctantly. "I suppose you're right. But I know something else we should do differently this time around."

"What?"

"Instead of betting on whether or not we can actually carry this off, let's just agree to have a big celebration after it's all over. Just you and me!"

"Okay. Banana splits again? I hear Fozzy's makes a great one."

"No . . . How about hot fudge sundaes this time? After all, variety is the spice of life."

"You've got a deal! We'll treat each other to hot fudge sundaes, right after the dedication of the monument. That's the very last event, isn't it? On Sunday afternoon."

"You realize what we've just done, don't you?" Susan was smiling impishly.

Chris just stared at her, puzzled. "No, Sooz. What have we just done?"

Her twin threw back her head and laughed. "We've just christened this little caper of ours. We'll call it 'The Hot Fudge Sunday Affair'!"

Three

The clear July sky, just deepening to a rich shade of cobalt blue, had become alive with fiery bursts of color. With great fanfare they exploded, one after another, red and green and blue and gold. They jubilantly cascaded through the air, then faded, only to be replaced by even more streaming colors.

It was the night before Centennial Week, and the long-awaited celebration was being kicked off with an impressive display of fireworks the likes of which the residents of Whittington had never seen before. It appeared that the whole town had come out to see them. They stood everywhere, on back porches and front lawns, on rooftops and fence posts, in the park, the school yards, and the sidewalks. Their necks were craned toward the sky. Everyone seemed to be enjoying them.

Everyone, that is, except for Felicia Harris.

In fact, she had refused to budge from her bedroom that entire evening. Her father, the mayor of Whittington, had insisted, growing so angry at her contrariness that his face and neck turned the same bright shade of red as his scarlet necktie, donned especially for the occasion. Her mother, elegant in her pink linen suit, had pleaded with her, saying it wouldn't look good if the mayor's family showed up for the occasion minus their youngest daughter. Even her sisters had gotten into the act. Heather had offered to lend her her white angora sweater if she'd agree to come. Jessica just shrugged and told her she was acting like a baby. But Felicia was a stubborn seventeen-year-old. She'd insisted she'd have no part in it, and she had absolutely no intention of changing her mind.

So she stayed home, alone. While the rest of her family was off enjoying the fireworks display, she planned to spend the evening pouting. Still, she couldn't resist a little peak. If she stood at the south window of her bedroom on the third floor of the Harrises' Victorian home and leaned out just a bit, she could get a glimpse of it. She had to admit that the display was breathtaking. But instead of cheering her up, it only made her feel worse.

Angrily she looked around her bedroom. The first thing that caught her eye was her teddy bear, lying across her bed, just as it had ever since she was two years old. Without a moment's hesitation, she picked it up and hurled it across the room. But even her temper tantrum failed. The stuffed bear simply landed in the wicker chair. It looked as comfortable there as it had on the bed. In fact, it looked as if it even *preferred* it there.

It was an exquisite bedroom. Or at least she had thought so until lately. The summer before, Felicia had announced to her family that her favorite color was yellow. Immediately her bedroom had been redone in yellow. The wallpaper was the color of daffodils. The bedspread, curtains, and cushions on the wicker chair were all made of fabric printed with sprigs of yellow flowers against a white background. Even the lampshades and throw rugs were yellow. She had adored this room. But tonight nothing seemed right.

And all because that other girl, that . . . that Christine Pratt or whatever her name was, had been chosen to be queen of Centennial Week. Instead of *her*. Instead of Felicia Harris, the mayor's daughter.

Felicia was, in her own eyes, the obvious choice. She was a natural. And she had been expecting to be picked ever since she had first heard rumors of the Centennial Committee choosing a local queen and king to reign over the festivities. And then, just a few weeks before, she heard the news. Not only did it make no sense. It simply wasn't *fair*.

Resolutely, Felicia strode over to the mirror hung above her dresser, encased in a yellow wicker frame. The girl looking back at her was confident, poised, sophisticated. Pretty, too, with her waist-length blond hair, gray-blue eyes, and fragile features. Exactly the right kind of girl to represent the town of Whittington. Its citizens. Its young people. To be the queen of Centennial Week.

The fact that Felicia spent very little time in Whittington didn't matter to her very much. Ever since she was twelve, she had chosen to go to a boarding school a hundred miles away. After all, where else could she learn horseback riding—in fact, have it included as part of her normal school day, just like math and English? Certainly not here! Not in a place like Whittington!

But having few ties to the town and not a single real friend there didn't seem very important. All Felicia knew was that there was something she'd wanted—and she hadn't gotten it.

For the hundredth time in the past three weeks, she opened up the old copy of the *Whittington Herald* dated June 30. On the front page, in the bottom-right corner, were two small grainy photographs. One was of a boy, posing with Whittington High's football coach. The other was a girl, about her age, smiling winningly at the camera. It looked like a candid shot, taken at a game or after school. For the school yearbook, perhaps. Above was the caption "King and Queen Chosen for Centennial Week."

The article below was short, really just a paragraph. And it said very little besides the names of the boy and girl selected and the reasons they'd been chosen. Jeffrey Miller, the newspaper said, had scored more touchdowns the autumn before than any other student in the school's history. And Christine Pratt had written an extensive research paper on the history of Whittington. There wasn't much information other than that.

But it was enough for Felicia.

"I'll get you, Christine Pratt," she muttered, folding up the newspaper and putting it back into her dresser drawer. "Starting tomorrow, I'm going to make a point of spoiling things for you. *No one* gets away with something like this!"

Four

Chris stood outside the entrance of City Hall, trying to convince herself that there was no reason in the world to be nervous. It was Monday, the first day of Centennial Week. She knew she looked perfect in her light blue flowered sundress with its matching scarf draped around her neck and shoulders in the flattering way her twin had devised.

And she certainly felt comfortable enough in this building. Just a few months earlier she had spent countless hours there as she researched her report after school and on Saturday mornings, poking around the vast collection of deeds, birth certificates, and other records that were stored in the basement.

As for the town over which she was about to reign, she'd lived in Whittington ever since she was born. Every street, house, and building was familiar to her. Over and over she reminded herself that today was going to be fun. But try as she did, she couldn't manage to get the butterflies in her stomach to stop the frantic beating of their wings.

Finally she took a deep breath and strode inside the building, muttering "Here goes!" under her breath. As she'd been instructed by the letter she received back in June, she went upstairs to report to the mayor's office.

She'd never actually been in Mayor Harris's office before. The reception area was impressive, with its soft brown leather furniture, thick carpeting, and a huge desk, behind which sat an attractive young woman with long dark hair and round eyeglasses with red frames.

Sitting on the edge of the leather couch was a boy about her age, dressed in a navy-blue blazer, white shirt, and red-white-and-blue–striped tie. His blond hair was still wet from his morning shower, but a small cowlick at the crown of his head popped up defiantly.

She immediately recognized him as Jeff Miller, her "king." She had never really talked to him at school; after all, he was a year ahead of her. But Chris knew who he was. Who didn't, with his incredible football record? She was relieved to see that he looked as nervous as she felt. "Hi," she said to both Jeff and the woman behind the desk. She was thinking that that was hardly a fitting greeting for a queen who was meeting her king for the very first time. But for the moment she couldn't think of anything else to say.

"Hi," Jeff returned with a bashful smile.

"Oh, you must be Christine. I'm Ann Benson, Mayor Harris's secretary." She came over and shook her hand. "It's so nice to meet you. And congratulations!"

"Thank you." Chris was starting to feel a bit better.

"I read that research project of yours. It was great. You must have spent a lot of time going through all those ancient town records in that musty old basement of ours! How did you every know where to begin? I don't think anyone else has dared to venture down there for years!"

Before Chris could answer, a much deeper voice interrupted. "Well, well, well. You must be Christine and Jeffrey. I'm Mayor Harris. Welcome and congratulations!" With great formality, he shook both their hands. "We've got a busy day ahead of us. We're going to . . . hmmm." His forehead furrowed, and he looked pleadingly at Ann. "What exactly *do* we have on for today, Ms. Benson?"

"I've typed up your exact itinerary." She handed him a sheet of paper with the day's schedule clearly laid out for him. Chris could barely suppress a giggle.

"Fine. But first we have to wait until my daughter gets here. I'm afraid she's invited herself along on our expedition this morning." Almost to himself, he mused, "Funny, ask any of the city council members, and they'll tell you what a hard-nose I am. But when it comes to Felicia, she always seems to get around me somehow."

Felicia sauntered in then. She looked as if being concerned about the possibility of keeping the others waiting was the last thing on her mind. Chris loved her own flowered sundress. But Felicia's white linen dress looked like something out of

Vogue magazine, and Chris suddenly felt frumpy. Or at least as if she were dressed like a little girl instead of a sophisticated young woman.

But she tried to be friendly. "Hello, Felicia," she said with a warm smile. "I'm Christine Pratt. And this is . . ."

"Yes, I know who you are." Felicia's steely blue eyes appraised her coldly. Chris was afraid she disapproved of the way she was dressed or the way she looked. She had no way of knowing that the older girl was having exactly the opposite reaction.

The mayor's daughter was much nicer to Jeff. She flashed him a huge smile and cocked her head flirtatiously. "And I *certainly* know who *you* are," she cooed. "Why, who doesn't? You're a positive *celebrity* in this town. And I happen to be a real football fan."

Jeff was turning a bright shade of red. Chris actually felt sorry for him.

"You know, I've been following your football career for ages. It seems that every time I look in the newspaper, there's your picture, along with some glowing report on how you just won another game for Whittington High."

Felicia suddenly turned to her father. "Well, Daddy," she said with great impatience, "what on earth are we waiting for? If we don't get moving, we're going to be late!"

As the foursome went out the front entrance, their schedule for the day tucked away safely in Mayor Harris's pocket, Chris was overcome with excitement. She was about to begin her first day as queen of Centennial Week! Even Felicia, chattering away beside her, couldn't put a damper on her enthusiasm. And when a sleek black limousine pulled up in front and a uniformed chauffeur jumped out to open the car door, she thought she was going to burst.

Wait until I tell Susan! was all she could think.

As their chauffeur for the week, Thomas, helped her inside the blue velour–covered backseat, Chris really did feel like royalty. This was turning out even better than her wildest dreams.

Their first stop was the new town library, an important-looking red brick building right across the street from the high school. Chris knew that Susan had been anticipating its opening with glee, and she wished it were *her* turn today so that she could be at the dedication. But as soon as she went inside, she became so engrossed in what was going on that she forgot all about her twin.

Everything in the library was brand-new. It even *smelled* new, Chris noted, inhaling deeply. Moss-green carpeting, big tables and comfortable chairs, rows of wooden shelves that seemed to go on forever. And, of course, books everywhere. There was even a special children's section. It had tiny tables and chairs, painted bright colors like red and yellow and blue, and the walls were painted with balloons and giant animals. It was such a pleasant place that Chris found herself actually looking forward to spending time here, reading and study-ing.

The main reading room was filled with people. What seemed like hundreds of men and women were standing around and chatting, drinking coffee and eating donuts served from a table in the back near the magazine section. While Chris was still debating whether or not it was appropriate for a queen to gorge herself on donuts, Felicia and her father disappeared. Even Jeff got lost in the crowd. So she wandered around by herself, looking for someone to talk to.

As she studied the faces around her more carefully, she began to recognize some of the people there. She had seen some of them in the local newspaper. Some had even been on television. She realized that these were some of the town's most prominent citizens. And so she was surprised and flattered when they all seemed anxious to meet *her*.

"So *you're* Christine," said Katherine Marshall, a member of the council known for the strides she had made in improving the Whittington school system. Years earlier, Ms. Marshall had insisted that computers were the wave of the future. Despite a great deal of resistance from both the school board and a band of skeptical parents, she had managed to acquire computers for each school. "I haven't had a chance to read your research paper yet, but everyone says it's just wonderful. Tell me: How did you decide to study local history? So few young people today seem to be interested in the local scene. Certainly, they're anxious to change the world, but they tend to think in terms of state, or even federal government. . . ."

"You must be our new queen." A jovial-looking man grinned at her. "I'm Ed Winters, chief of the fire department. You know, someone was telling me you discovered that Whittington was one of the first towns in the area to institute a salaried fire brigade.

Everyone else was using volunteers. Can you tell me more about that?"

It was demanding being a celebrity. But Chris loved it.

The nervousness that had plagued her earlier that morning had vanished. She found it easy to chat with these people. They were all so interested in talking to her about her research project. She was glad she'd taken the time to review it. She spoke easily and knowledgeably about her subject. In fact, she realized with satisfaction, this was something she probably knew more about than anyone else in the room. She loved being in the limelight. Even noting that Felicia was glaring at her from across the room failed to daunt her good spirits.

The mayor gave a short speech, dedicating the library to the citizens of Whittington and emphasizing the importance of reading and education. Afterward, he introduced the king and queen, and the town librarian presented Chris with a bouquet of flowers. Then Chris and the others hurried off to their next appointment, leaving behind the others to explore the building and finish off the coffee and donuts.

As they walked to the car, Jeff made a point of coming over to Chris's side.

"Hey, you were quite a hit in there!" he teased her.

"Oh, I was just being friendly."

"Don't be so modest! You were the belle of the ball. You had everyone charmed. I think the fire chief wanted to ask you for a date."

Chris burst out laughing at the images that

immediately popped into her mind. "I suppose we could go to the movies in a fire truck."

"Probably. But they'd never let the Dalmatians into the theater." Then Jeff grew serious. "Listen, Chris, let's try to stick closer together next time, okay?"

"Good idea. That way if anyone asks us something tricky or either of us starts losing his cool, we can help each other out."

Jeff looked puzzled. "Well . . . that's not exactly what I meant."

Chris glanced over at him and saw that he was blushing. It occurred to her that what he was saying was not that he wanted her to help him keep the conversation going in his role as king but that he *liked* being with her. And, she realized, she felt exactly the same way. She began to glow. The rewards of being queen were turning out to be even more than she had hoped for.

The rest of the day was a whirlwind of fun. Besides being queen, it was like a long, if unusual, date with Jeff. The remainder of the morning was taken up by the ribbon cutting of the building site for the new elementary school. Chris was amused by the sight of all the workers posed by their cranes and other machinery, impatiently waiting for the mayor to cut the blue ribbon strung across the gate so they could get to work. A luncheon given by the local chapter of the Lions' Club followed. In the afternoon there was an exhibition of the 4-H Club's projects and the Grand Opening of a small shopping mall.

Along with the others, Chris was whisked from place to place in the limousine. She had barely enough time to comb her hair between events. It was tiring, but she enjoyed every minute. Everyone was anxious to meet her and to talk about her research on the town's history. She felt very, very important. Exactly the way a queen was *supposed* to feel, she decided.

It wasn't until the middle of the afternoon that she remembered that she was only queen for the day. Tomorrow it would be Susan's turn. And she had promised to fill her in on every little detail of how she had spent the morning and afternoon. As they were driving out of the parking lot of the new shopping mall, with Felicia chattering away about her school and her favorite horse without noticing that no one was listening, Chris reached into her purse and brought out the small pad of paper she had tucked inside just for this purpose.

"What's that?" Jeff asked curiously. "Are you starting a collection of autographs? I suppose you'll want mine first." Pretending reluctance, he reached for the pad.

Chris laughed. "Not exactly. Actually, I've been meaning to take notes on what I do this week."

"A diary?"

"Sort of. After all," she explained hastily, "this is all pretty exciting. I want to make sure I don't forget a single detail."

Jeff looked doubtful.

"Besides, I might want to write about this experience someday. For the school paper, I mean. Or a school project."

"That reminds me," said Mayor Harris. Felicia looked annoyed at having her discourse on her wonderful friends at school cut off. "Starting in

another day or so, we're going to be having some
company on our little expeditions. Someone *other*
than Felicia, I mean," he added meaningfully. His
daughter just scowled and stared out the window.
"There'll be a reporter coming along with us.
Someone from the *Whittington Herald*. A young
man by the name of Eric Caulfield, I believe."

"You mean he'll be covering Centennial Week?"
Chris asked.

"Well, yes. But I understand that his main focus
will be the two of you. A human interest approach
to the town's honorary king and queen. See, you'll
be even bigger celebrities than you already are by
the time his big feature article on Whittington's two
most prominent teen-agers comes out."

Felicia's scowl was deeper than ever. But she
remained silent.

Chris, too, was silent. She was lost in thought.
Worried thought.

A real reporter, accompanying the king and
queen everywhere. Asking questions, taking notes,
watching and listening. With someone scrutinizing
the queen so carefully, being with her every minute
of the day, would she and Susan ever make it to Hot
Fudge Sunday? For the first time since she and her
twin had agreed to the plan, Chris began to have
serious doubts.

Even so, she wasn't about to back down. Not
now, when Susan hadn't even had a chance at being
queen yet. That would really be unfair. Especially
since it was all turning out to be so much fun.

"Where are we going now?" she asked, putting
away her note pad and vowing to record every
detail of her day the very first free moment she had.

"How does this sound?" The mayor turned to her and Jeff and grinned. "The Adult Education Center is having a fair, and we're the honored guests."

"Oh, Daddy, that sounds so dull." Felicia pouted.

"Maybe you think so. But the Advanced Baking class has been working madly all weekend to make their best cakes and cookies for us to sample. I hope you have a sweet tooth, Chris," he added with a wink.

Christine Pratt just laughed.

Five

"Now don't forget, Sooz. We had lobster salad at the Lions' Club luncheon. And I had, let's see, a Coke. Jeff ate three rolls. With gobs of butter."

Chris was in Susan's bedroom, pacing back and forth and delivering a monologue as her sister got dressed. She wanted to be sure she didn't leave out a single fact, name, or event about the day before, and she had been talking nonstop ever since seven that morning. "Oh, one more thing. It was the *fire* chief, not the police chief, that I met yesterday, at the dedication of the new library. His name was . . . oh, gee, I can't remember. Ed something, I think.

"And don't forget that Mayor Harris's secretary's name is Ann Benson. She has long black hair and glasses. But you can't miss her. She sits right in the waiting room outside the mayor's office.

"Oh, I just thought of something else. Did I mention that the mayor's daughter's name is Felicia?"

33

"Only about six times," groaned Susan. "Relax, Chris! I'm not worried; why should you be? I have every confidence that I've been briefed on every single detail of your first day as queen."

It was Tuesday morning. In just a few minutes Susan would be off to take her place as queen of Centennial Week—*and* as Christine Pratt. It was hard to tell which of the twins was more nervous. But while Chris was a bundle of energy, Susan was acting calm. Her restraint, however, came only from being afraid of letting her apprehension show. If she did, she feared she'd never manage to get herself out the door.

"If anything goes wrong, just wing it," Chris whispered as she started down the stairs.

"I'll be *fine!*" Susan insisted. She only wished she believed it.

"All set, Chris?" her father asked as she came downstairs.

So far so good, Susan thought. At least I've managed to convince *one* person that I'm really Chris!

Her sister had done her hair and applied her makeup for her, just to make sure their game wasn't found out because of some minor detail. She had even drawn a tiny beauty mark on her left cheek, something that had almost given them away the first time they had tried trading places. And she was wearing one of her twin's favorite outfits, a black-and-white–striped tee-shirt dress with a red belt, a string of red beads, and a pair of earrings that looked like big red buttons.

"You look very nice, dear," her mother commented. She, too, failed to realize that it was Susan she was addressing, not Chris. Susan could feel her confidence soaring. Perhaps this was going to work after all.

It wasn't until she was standing at the entrance of the City Hall that she recognized how many gaps there were in the hasty education she'd received that morning and the evening before. For example, she knew that she was supposed to report to the mayor's office and that it was on the third floor . . . but where were the elevators? She certainly couldn't ask anyone. And how would she know if she was talking to Ann Benson, the mayor's secretary, or to someone else? Her confidence was fading. But it was too late to turn back now. Hiding her nervousness so well that even she was impressed, she strode inside the cavernous lobby of the building.

Fortunately, she found Mayor Harris's office without mishap. And no one seemed to notice her anyway. The employees of City Hall were too intent on getting to work on time and catching up on the latest gossip to pay any attention to her. It wasn't until she went into the mayor's office that she met up with her first challenge of the day.

There was a woman sitting behind the desk typing. She smiled at Susan as she walked in. But she distinctly remembered Chris saying that Ann Benson had long black hair and glasses. This woman had short hair and no glasses.

"Hello there," the woman greeted her. She continued looking at Susan expectantly.

"Hello." Susan didn't know whether to introduce herself or to assume that this was Ms.

Benson—who of course already knew Christine Pratt.

Her sister's parting words echoed through her brain. *If anything goes wrong, just wing it!*

Susan took a deep breath. "Well, I'm back for my second day as queen of Centennial Week!" she said gaily.

The woman behind the desk broke into a huge smile. "Then I guess you had a good time yesterday, Chris. By the way, how do you like my hair? I had it cut last night. Unfortunately, I left my eyeglasses at the hairdresser's. I'll pick them up at lunchtime, but in the meantime, I've got a tough morning ahead of me. Why, I wasn't even sure if it was you when you walked in just now!"

A wave of relief rushed over Susan. "Your hair looks terrific, Ms. Benson."

"Now, I told you yesterday, Chris. Please call me Ann."

"Sorry. Guess I forgot."

"That's okay. I'm sure you have enough to remember!"

If she only knew! Susan thought ruefully.

"By the way, Mayor Harris will be out in a minute. And you'll probably be pleased to know that Felicia won't be joining you today. The mayor finally put his foot down. Now, if you'll excuse me, I really have to get this report typed." She squinted at the page before her as she went back to her typing.

This is going to be a long day, thought Susan, plopping into the comfortable brown leather couch. But at the very least, I'll learn a valuable lesson in diplomacy. Maybe this experience will even teach me not to put my foot in my mouth quite so often in the future.

When Jeff Miller hurried in a few minutes later, Susan had no problem recognizing him. The school's football star was as familiar to her as he was to Chris and everyone else at Whittington High.

"Hi, Jeff!" she said brightly.

"How's my queen today? Looking good, I see." He sat down on the couch next to her. A bit too close, Susan couldn't help noticing. "Now, Chris, don't forget what I told you yesterday."

Susan just smiled wanly. She had no idea what he was talking about—yet she could tell by his conspiratorial tone that she *should* know. It seemed to be important. She wondered if she should pretend to know . . . or take a risk by trying to find out. She decided that this sounded too important simply to let it pass by.

"To tell you the truth, Jeff," she said, "yesterday was such a long, exhausting day that I'm not sure I remember *anything*. What exactly did you say?"

Jeff looked at her quizzically. Susan's heart sank. But then he burst out laughing. "Yeah, I guess you're right. A lot *did* happen to us yesterday, didn't it? Well, I'm talking about you and me planning to stick close together all day. So we won't get separated, the way we did at the library."

"Oh, yes. Of course. And you're absolutely right."

Another small victory.

When the mayor finally emerged from his office, Susan held her breath. But he barely glanced at her. He simply said, "Good morning, kids. All set for

another day? By the way, Ann, see if you can get
Henry Clark on the phone this morning. I'll have to
cancel our golf game tomorrow. Tell him I'll call to
reschedule after this week is over." He smiled
apologetically at Susan and Jeff. "This Centennial
Week is certainly keeping us all busy, isn't it?"

By then all of Susan's confidence had returned.
She had no problem convincing anyone that she
was Chris. Not the mayor, not Ann Benson—not
even Jeff.

Now, she thought, all I have to do is be careful
not to slip up for the rest of the day.

Being queen of Centennial Week was exhilarat-
ing. Susan was as thrilled as her twin had been
when Thomas, the chauffeur, helped her into the
long black limousine. And as they drove from place
to place, their arrival was inevitably greeted with a
great deal of fanfare: cheers, crepe-paper streamers
and balloons, people crowding around and snap-
ping their pictures. When they visited the firehouse,
a small group of firemen in red band uniforms broke
into a rousing march as they pulled up. And while
she was inhibited by shyness at first, it didn't take
long to realize that everyone was so excited over
Centennial Week, so pleased to be a part of it, that
they were happy just to shake her hand.

Things proceeded smoothly until it was time for
the king and queen to judge an art show given by
the town's day camp. As she filed through the
exhibit, viewing artwork done by children aged
four to fourteen in every possible medium from
wood to paint to papier-mâché, she became totally
engrossed in examining each piece.

"This is so much fun!" she bubbled to Jeff.

"You know, art is my favorite subject at school. I'm even thinking of going on to art school after high school."

Jeff's response snapped her back to her present situation. "I had no idea, Chris. Why, I didn't even know you *took* art."

"Oh. Um . . ." Susan could feel herself turning red. She had been so wrapped up in enjoying the art show that she'd completely forgotten she was playing the part of her twin! And now she had said something that could very well get Chris in trouble the next day. "Well, I don't actually take *classes* at school. It's just sort of a hobby. I like to fiddle around with it after school."

She looked over at Jeff timidly, hoping her answer hadn't sounded too odd. But he was barely listening. Instead, he was absorbed in a particularly imaginative display of watercolors. Even so, Susan vowed to say as little as possible for the rest of the day. That had been an awfully close call!

After lunch, given by the local Girl Scouts and their troop leaders at the American Legion Hall, the mayor suddenly said to Susan and Jeff, "Well, I'm afraid I'll have to leave you two on your own for the rest of the day. Centennial Week is all well and good, but I've still got a city government to run. There's a council meeting this afternoon, and I've got to be there. But Thomas knows the schedule for the rest of the day. I'm sure you'll both do fine. Have fun!"

"At last we're alone!" Jeff said, leaning back against the plush blue velour of the backseat. Casually he draped his arm around Susan's shoulders.

She stiffened. What on earth did Jeff think he was doing?

But then she remembered that he thought it was *Chris* he was with.

Oh, dear, she thought. Chris had never mentioned anything about her and Jeff being interested in each other.

But even if she had said they were, that wouldn't make this situation any easier. How would she, Susan, get out of this gracefully, without ruining things for her sister? This was something that she had never even considered!

Susan thought fast. And then she had an idea. In her most teasing Chris voice, she said, "Now, Jeffrey Miller, I think you're forgetting that you're a public figure. You have a responsibility to your position." Playfully but firmly she removed his arm from her shoulders, then pretended to smooth her dress. "Honestly!" she went on with mock horror. "Have you ever seen Prince Charles and Lady Di carry on in public?"

She hoped Jeff would simply laugh it off. But he didn't. Instead, he acted as if he were hurt.

"Boy, I don't understand you, Chris." He pouted. "I keep getting mixed signals from you. You're like hot and cold running water. And here I thought you really liked me!"

Angry and bewildered, he slid across the seat, as far away from her as he could get. Thomas, the chauffeur, glanced at his two passengers through the rearview mirror. But he said nothing.

For the rest of the day, Jeff remained quiet and distant. Even Susan's attempts at making cheerful conversation couldn't bring him out of his bad mood. And at the end of the afternoon, he hurried off without even bothering to say good-bye.

Oh, no. *Now* look at what I've done. No wonder Jeff is confused, with Chris acting friendly one day and me being standoffish the next. And tomorrow it's Chris's turn again. He's going to think his queen has a split personality.

And I guess she does, Susan thought morosely. Much more than he'll ever know!

Six

It was already past five when Susan stumbled into Ann Benson's office to use the telephone. She was glad it was deserted. The door to the mayor's office was closed, signifying that he had already gone home for the day. And Ann's desk was empty, her light turned off, her typewriter covered up for the night.

Grateful for the chance to be alone, Susan sank onto the soft couch. The red shoes that Chris had insisted were crucial for the outfit she was wearing were molded to her twin's feet, not hers, and they had been reminding her of that fact all day. She slid them off and wiggled her toes. It was a relief to be able to relax, to lean back, to close her eyes. She needed just a moment's rest before calling her father and asking him to pick her up. Just a moment . . .

The next thing she knew, Susan was being dragged out of a deep sleep. Someone was shaking her shoulder gently, saying "Wake up! Hey, whoever you are, I think you'd better wake up!"

Susan opened her eyes and found herself face-to-face with a congenial-looking young man.

"Camping out?" he asked teasingly. His green eyes were twinkling, and he was grinning at her as if the two of them shared some wonderful secret.

"What? Where am I? Oh, no; what time is it?"

"Five-thirty or so. Is that when your nap time is usually over, Sleeping Beauty, or did I wake you up too soon?"

"Five-thirty! I've got to get home!" Susan sat up, trying to blink the tiredness out of her eyes. "I have to call my father."

"Are you sure I shouldn't call a security guard? I mean how do I know I'm not dealing with some hardened criminal who's hiding out here in Mayor Harris's office?"

Susan looked at the stranger carefully. On second glance, he looked as if he wasn't much older than she was. And his reddish-brown hair, merry green eyes, and sprinkling of light freckles made him look even younger. "Who are you?"

The boy extended his hand with mock formality. "Eric Caulfield, at your service. Reporter-at-large for none other than the *Herald*, Whittington's finest—and only—newspaper."

"Oh, no! You're the reporter I heard about!"

"Well, I must say I've had friendlier first meetings before. But I promise not to hold it against you. Speaking of which, who are *you*?"

Susan stopped herself just as she was about to say "Susan Pratt," her usual automatic response. Instead, she took a deep breath and said, "I'm Christine Pratt."

"Ah-ha! So *you're* the reigning queen! I didn't

realize I was in the presence of royalty. If I did, I would have knelt down or asked permission to speak . . . or at least asked for your autograph."

Susan was fully awake by now, and she couldn't help laughing. "You're not at all what I expected."

"Uh-oh. And here I was hoping to impress everyone in this town with my worldliness. Not to mention my charm."

"What do you mean? Don't you live here in Whittington?"

"I do now. But just for the summer. You see, I just finished my freshman year of college, and I managed to wangle my way onto the staff of the *Herald* for the summer. My first job as a reporter. I figured working for a small-town paper was a good way to get my feet wet. Easier to learn my way around the business, too."

"How's it going so far?"

"Well . . ." For the first time, Eric seemed a trifle unsure of himself. "To be perfectly honest, my reporting career has been less than stellar so far. All they've let me cover were a dog show and a kindergarten graduation. Not that I didn't do my best to make them both sound like the social events of the century." Eric sighed. "At least I'm sure I created some loyal readers in the canine world."

"Poor thing!" chuckled Susan. "And now you're covering Centennial Week."

Eric brightened. "Yes! This is my first big chance! I plan to show what I can do with this assignment. Really go to town."

Susan was immediately put on her guard. "What do you mean?"

"For one thing, I want to do a thorough, probing

analysis of what makes Whittington's honorary king and queen tick. That means *you*, my dear. I'm doing a big feature story for this Sunday's paper—on you! You'll be famous! Not that you aren't already, of course . . ."

Susan's heart sank.

"Anyway, I plan to be with you and King Jeff every minute of every day, from tomorrow morning until my deadline, midnight on Saturday."

Uh-oh. I'd better talk to Chris *immediately*, Susan thought. It might be time to reevaluate the Hot Fudge Sunday Affair. "By the way, Eric, exactly what kind of reporter do you want to be? Are you interested in sportswriting or human interest or . . ."

"Oh, no. Nothing like that. I want to be an investigative reporter. You know, the kind who really gets involved in a story, who gets to the bottom of things. Who exposes fraud and corruption. I intend to have a reputation for leaving no stone unturned," he added proudly.

Inwardly Susan was groaning. "Excuse me. I'd better go call my family."

"I can take a hint," Eric said with a grin. "I'll be on my way now, and you're free to have your privacy." He stood up to leave. "Actually, I just stopped in to see if Mayor Harris was around. But I guess I'll catch up with him tomorrow. I'll have plenty of time then." He started for the door. "Yes, sir. This is going to be fun. And I'm looking forward to getting to know you better, too, Queen Christine. I intend to find out exactly what makes Christine Pratt tick!"

Despite her apprehensions about having a reporter around for the next few days, Susan had to admit that the idea of it was not totally unpleasant. There was something engaging about Eric Caulfield—his cheerfulness, his talkativeness, his laughing green eyes. She was torn between wanting to spend time with him and protecting the secret that she and her twin shared.

Well, at least I won't have to worry about it again until Thursday, thought Susan. Tomorrow it's Chris's turn to be queen.

Susan had planned to make only a short telephone call, simply asking her father to come pick her up at City Hall. But when Chris answered, she couldn't resist telling her the latest news.

"Hi, it's me, Chris." Susan kept her voice low, just in case someone walked by in the hall. "Would you please tell Daddy I'm ready to come home?"

"Sure, Sooz. Hey, how did it go today?"

"To be perfectly honest, I'm not too sure. There were a couple of awfully tense moments. And I'm afraid something happened with Jeff. I'll have to tell you all about it as soon as I get home. . . ."

"But you made it! You know, after you left this morning, I thought of a million things I'd forgotten to tell you. I was worried all day."

"I'll fill you in later. But there is one major complication I think you should know about right away."

"Uh-oh. What's up?"

"Well, remember that reporter Mayor Harris told you about yesterday?"

"Yes?"

"He showed up today. He's nice and all"—Susan

wasn't quite ready to tell her sister *how* nice—"but I'm kind of worried about him."

"Oh, no. The snoopy type, huh?"

"Chris, he wants to be an investigative reporter when he finishes college! You know, the kind who uncovers all the skeletons that politicians and everybody else have hidden away in their closets."

"I suppose that goes for honorary royalty, too." Chris sighed.

"It sure does! In fact, he's planning an in-depth feature article for this Sunday's paper, on none other than Christine Pratt. He said he wants to find out what makes her tick."

Chris thought for a minute. "This will make things more difficult, of course . . . but more of a challenge! We can beat this, Sooz. No sweat!"

"Chris! You sound like you think we should continue! Do you still think we can manage to take turns being queen of Centennial Week? That I can still pretend to be *you* half the time—and carry it off without anyone finding out?"

"Absolutely! We knew when we decided to do this that we'd be under watch all the time. That makes it all the more fun. Look at it this way: this reporter will just help keep us on our toes."

"I wish I could be as optimistic as you are."

"Come on, Sooz. Where's the old Pratt spirit? I can't believe that any twin of mine would be afraid to rise to a challenge!"

"Well . . ."

"We'll talk about it later, okay? And don't worry! We've both been doing fine so far, and there's no reason why that should change. Right?"

"Right." It wasn't until Susan had hung up the

phone and was scurrying out the door to meet her father that she muttered, "That is, I *hope* she's right!"

Felicia Harris was wearing a smug smile as she gently hung up the telephone. So Christine Pratt had a twin sister! And the two girls were taking turns pretending to be Chris so they could both enjoy being queen. That was interesting information. *Very* interesting information, indeed!

She was sitting in her father's office, behind the closed door. After running some errands in town, she'd stopped in to say hello to her father. But it was almost five by the time she arrived, and he and his secretary were both gone for the day. Since she knew where Ann kept the spare key hidden, she had no problem slipping inside—supposedly just to cool off in his air-conditioned office for a few minutes.

But then she'd heard someone come in, and she'd waited. She had a hunch that something interesting might happen. And the flirtatious interlude between the queen of Centennial Week and the fledgling reporter who was about to cover her short reign was no disappointment.

But it was nothing compared to the telephone conversation that Felicia had just listened in on.

So Chris and Susan Pratt were trying their hand at a little deception, were they? And they seemed so confident that they could get away with it. That was the part Felicia found so irritating. Imagine, the two of them believing they could actually pull the wool over everyone's eyes. The mayor, the reporter . . . even her! It was mind-boggling.

Well, my little dears, thought Felicia as she

gathered up her things to go home, the week isn't over yet. Your little charade has just begun. And now that I'm onto you . . . well, let's just say that I plan to make sure your reign as queen of Centennial Week is something you won't soon forget!

Seven

The mood hovering over the kitchen table where Chris and Susan were having breakfast on Wednesday morning was quite different from the one of the two previous mornings. Whereas they had started the week filled with enthusiasm over the double adventure before them—being queen of Centennial Week *and* taking turns pretending to be the same person—they were now beginning to wonder if what they had set out to do was simply impossible.

By this point, even Chris was getting discouraged. She hadn't been too worried about the news of Eric Caulfield's arrival on the scene—and his contention that he intended to find out what made Christine Pratt tick. But once her twin told her what had happened with Jeff, she, too, had begun to experience doubts.

"I'm so sorry I messed things up with you and Jeff," Susan said as she buttered an English muffin. "I tried my best to wriggle my way out of it. And I thought that line about Prince Charles and Lady Di would do the trick. But he acted so . . . so *hurt*."

"I know. It wasn't your fault. Besides, I should have warned you that Jeff and I were on the verge of becoming more than just king and queen." Chris sighed and stared at her bowl of cereal, which she still hadn't touched. The corn flakes were quickly becoming soggy, threatening to sink to the bottom. But even watching their rapid demise failed to motivate her to eat anything. "Maybe I can straighten things out with him today."

"Then there's the reporter. He's *really* got me worried. Don't get me wrong; Eric is very nice. But he seems so dedicated to unearthing the truth!"

Just then their mother poked her head into the kitchen. "You'd better hurry, Chris," she said with a big smile. "It's almost time for you to leave. I'll tell your father you're just about ready."

Once she was out of earshot, Susan turned to Chris and said earnestly, "Well, one thing's for sure. I'm glad it's *your* turn to be queen today. I never thought I'd feel this way, but I need a break from being queen of Centennial Week. This is turning out to be more difficult than I ever expected."

"I'm sure it'll be fine," Chris said bravely as she stood up to leave. "After all, I *am* the real Chris Pratt. I don't have anything to hide from Eric Caulfield. As for Jeff . . . well, just keep your fingers crossed!"

Susan resolved to spend the rest of the day doing just that.

Despite her attempts at optimism, Chris was filled with apprehension as she waltzed into the mayor's office. Just as she'd expected, Jeff's greet-ing was icy.

"Well, look who's here. It's Whittington's own Lady Di." His tone was so cold that even Ann Benson glanced up, obviously curious about this sudden change in the way the king and queen were getting along. Up until now, they had seemed so friendly that she had wondered if a summer ro-mance was budding right before her eyes.

"Excuse me," she said, diplomatically slipping away from the office. "I have to pick up a few things in the supply room. I'll be back in five minutes. Oh, and by the way, you kids are on your own again today. Mayor Harris is going to be tied up with meetings all day."

"Jeff, I'd like to talk to you about yesterday." Chris sat down on the couch next to him. "I was hoping you'd understand that I didn't mean to be hot and cold, the way you described me." She hoped her sister's recitation of their conversation in the backseat of the limousine had been accurate. But Jeff seemed to know exactly what she was talking about. "The truth is, I take this business of being queen of Centennial Week very seriously. Sure, it's lots of fun, going around to different luncheons and parades and all. But we *are* in the spotlight. We're supposed to be symbols, in a way. You know, the youth of Whittington and all that. And to me that says we have to put our personal feelings aside for this week.

"Once it's all over, of course, you and I can go back to being ourselves, just Jeff Miller and Christine Pratt. But in the meantime . . ." She searched his face, anxious to see if what she was saying was making any sense to him.

"I suppose so." Jeff still didn't sound convinced.

Oh, dear. This is going to be a long day, thought Chris with a sigh. Well, it just so happens that I really do believe what I just said. I'd stick to it whether Susan and I were changing places or not. And if Jeff is the kind of boy who refuses to see things logically, then I guess I just misjudged him. Things wouldn't work out anyway.

Jeff was still thinking about what she'd just said a minute or two later when another boy appeared in the doorway. Chris immediately surmised that it was Eric Caulfield. Any doubts she might have had were immediately dispelled by his friendly introduction.

"Hello, again, Chris. And you must be Jeff Miller. I'm Eric Caulfield, reporter for the *Whittington Herald*. I'm covering Centennial Week for the paper. And as Chris here already knows, I'm especially interested in its two star players, King Jeff and Queen Christine."

"Hello, Eric." The two boys shook hands. But Chris had the feeling there was an undercurrent of tension running between them. It wasn't until Jeff spoke that she understood what it was all about.

"So," he said, eyeing Eric warily, "you and Chris already know each other?"

"We certainly do. We met last night." When Eric winked at her meaningfully, Chris was startled. But Jeff's eyes suddenly grew wide. He looked at Chris, then at Eric—and back at Chris again.

Chris suddenly realized what she was going to be up against for the rest of the day.

Oh, no! How am I ever going to convince Jeff that he and I are still on good terms—and at the same time let Eric know that the *other* Chris is interested in *him*? This really *is* becoming an impossible situation!

Well, she decided, I guess that for the rest of the day I'll just have to try to convince both Jeff *and* Eric that I like them. But I'd better be careful not to make either one of them jealous. . . .

She was beginning to understand exactly how her sister had felt the day before.

Chris was nervous all morning. Fortunately, their schedule was a busy one. As Thomas whisked the three of them from place to place in the limousine, there was little time for chitchat. Chris tried to keep a balance, being friendly to both Eric and Jeff, ignoring whatever bad feelings she sensed still existed between them. At the same time, she also tried to say as little about herself as possible. Still, she felt as if with every passing moment, she and Susan were getting in deeper and deeper.

Things proceeded relatively smoothly until early afternoon, as they drove from the Elks' Club luncheon to a reception at the town pool. Jeff suddenly turned to her and said, "So tell me about your interest in art."

Eric's ears immediately pricked up. "What's this? Whittington's queen is an artist?" Automatically he reached for his notebook.

"Well, I . . ." she stammered. So Susan had unwittingly mentioned her interest in art! And now Chris would have to fake her way through a conversation on painting. That, she knew, was something she could never pull off. "I dabble in it," she said hesitantly. "I'm not very good, of course. . . ."

"But you said yesterday that you wanted to go to art school!"

"She's probably just being modest." Eric was busily jotting something down in his little book. "I'll make a note about our queen's creative aspirations. That's just the kind of thing I need for my feature article! I'd like to find out more about it. . . ."

Chris didn't know what to do. She needed to distract them, to get Eric and Jeff off this topic of conversation. When the car lurched to a stop at a red light, she did the first thing that came to mind. She pretended the jolt had knocked her purse off her lap. Before anyone knew what was happening, a shower of makeup and change and other assorted items fell all over the backseat and the floor.

"Oh, no! *Now* look what I've done! I'm so clumsy sometimes. . . ."

The subject of art was forgotten as the three of them scrambled around the back of the limousine, retrieving pencils and mascara and pennies from every possible corner of the upholstery.

By the end of the day, Chris was exhausted—and totally discouraged.

Maybe Mom was right, she thought as Thomas drove into the circular driveway in front of City Hall. Maybe there *can* be only one queen.

She vowed to have a serious talk with her twin that very evening, right after dinner. As much as she hated to admit it, she was beginning to suspect that carrying through the Hot Fudge Sunday Affair for the rest of the week was simply impossible.

Even for that undauntable duo, Christine and Susan Pratt.

Eight

"So, Chris, how did it go today?" Mr. Pratt *helped* himself to a generous dollop of mashed potatoes, then passed the bowl on to Susan. "You've been the queen of Centennial Week for three days now. How are you enjoying it?"

Chris glanced at her twin sister warily. "Well, it's certainly never boring!"

But Susan was in a playful mood. "Come on, Chris. I bet you love every minute. For one thing, you're such a ham that I'm sure you must thrive on being in the spotlight. I, on the other hand, would undoubtedly find it difficult to go running around Whittington, meeting and greeting, acting as some sort of goodwill ambassador."

"Well, then, it's a good thing I was chosen, and not you!" By this point, Chris was wearing a huge grin. Even all the doubts she'd been having didn't keep her from appreciating the humor of the situation.

"Yes, good thing!" Susan agreed heartily. "Mom, could you please pass the carrots?"

"You never did tell us about yesterday," said Mrs. Pratt. "How was the art show at the day camp?"

Chris and Susan exchanged nervous glances. "It was, um, great. Really great."

"You know," Mrs. Pratt went on, "May McCormick's daughter Janice was supposed to be exhibiting some papier-mâché animals she made. She was quite proud of them, actually. Did you happen to see them?"

Chris earnestly studied her plate. "Uh, let's see . . . I don't remember *everything* I saw. . . ."

"Sure, you saw them," Susan interrupted. "Remember? You were telling me all about them last night. There was a huge orange lion with a mane made out of shredded newspaper and a blue-and-green giraffe with polka dots and a purple elephant."

"Oh, yes. Now I remember."

"Yes," Susan said matter-of-factly, "they were beautiful. At least, the way you described them to me."

"Did you choose them for first prize?" Mrs. Pratt asked eagerly. "It certainly sounds as if you were impressed with them."

"No, Chris chose two clay figures. They were part of a Zodiac series. They represented Gemini, the Twins. They were quite well done, weren't they, Chris?"

Chris gulped. "Very well done."

"Goodness, it sounds as if Susan remembers more of the details of the art show than you do,

Chris," Mr. Pratt observed. Chris and Susan both grew tense, but then he said, "Would someone pass me the rolls? These are really good! I don't remember ever having these before."

Relieved, the twins looked at each other and grinned.

After dinner, Chris and her mother went out to visit their neighbors who'd just had their kitchen redone and were anxious to show it off. Susan was upstairs, on her way to take a shower, when the telephone rang.

"I'll get it!" she called downstairs to her father. "Hello?"

"Hi! It's Eric Caulfield. How are you, Chris?"

It was not the first time that someone phoning the house had mistaken one sister for the other. But it was one of the few instances when the caller had no idea that there was a pair of twins at the Pratt's house. Since Eric had already assumed that he was talking to Chris, Susan decided that the safest thing to do was go along with his assumption.

"I'm fine, Eric. How are you?" She was aware that her voice had softened and that it was probably clear how pleased she was to hear from him.

"Fine. Listen, I wanted to ask you for a little favor. You know, you're so busy during the day that I feel like the only way I ever get to talk to you is on the run."

"They do keep me busy, don't they?"

"I'll say! So I was wondering if you and I could sit down together and talk. That way I can really do an in-depth interview. Find out more about things like your interest in art. You know, that deadline of mine is getting closer every minute, and I still don't feel as if I've gotten to know the *real* Christine Pratt."

And you're not about to, either, Susan thought, trying hard not to giggle at the irony of what he was saying. "Well, sure, Eric. That's a great idea. When were you thinking of getting together?"

"Are you free tonight?"

"Why, yes, I am, as a matter of fact." Susan found herself actually looking forward to playing the role of Christine Pratt again—especially if it involved spending the evening with Eric Caulfield. Even though it meant she would be subject to very close scrutiny.

"Great. How about if I stop over in about an hour?"

"Oh, no! Not here!" In a more controlled voice, she said, "No, that's not a very good idea." Not if my mother walks in with Chris and sees *me* being interviewed for the newspaper! "My, um, parents are having some friends over tonight for a little party, and, well, it'll just be easier if you and I meet somewhere else." Somewhere as far away from the house as possible!

"Okay. But where should we go? Frankly, I'm not all that familiar with Whittington yet."

"I know the perfect place."

Less than an hour later, Susan was sitting at a small white table at Fozzy's Ice Cream Parlor, waiting for Eric. It was such a pleasant place, with its pink-and-white-striped wallpaper, long marble counter running along one side, and elaborate wrought-iron tables and chairs that were reminiscent of an old-fashioned ice cream parlor, the kind

that was found on every Main Street of every small
town in America at the turn of the century.

And she was confident that she would have no
trouble passing as Chris. In fact, even though she
had decided to dress very casually, she had raided
her twin's closet and dresser. Wearing Chris's jeans
and lavender tee-shirt instead of her own clothes
gave her an extra burst of confidence. It helped her
get that much more involved in playing the part.
She'd even put two of her sister's purple barrettes in
her chestnut hair.

When she saw Eric appear in the doorway, scan
the crowd, and then break into a sincere grin once
he spotted her, Susan's heart did a flip-flop.

Calm down, she warned herself. This isn't a
date, remember? Not only is Eric Caulfied interested in you because you're the queen of Centennial
Week. He also thinks you're someone named
Christine Pratt!

Still, even the most cautious part of her had to
admit that he did look happy to see her. Much
happier than she would expect a reporter to look as
he was meeting someone who was simply the
subject of an article he was writing.

"Hi, Chris. Glad you could make it. This looks
like a nice place."

"Especially if you're as big an ice cream fan as I
am."

"Are you kidding? Ice cream is my middle
name. I just hope they have pistachio. There's
nothing like pistachio ice cream in a hot fudge
sundae. Do you like sundaes?"

Susan smiled mysteriously. "Let's just say that

I'm not really in the mood for one tonight. I think I'll stick to a vanilla milk shake."

After they ordered, Susan folded her hands on the table and looked at Eric expectantly. "Well?"

"Well, what?"

"Aren't you going to take out a pad and start asking me a million questions and writing down every word I say?"

"Oh, yeah. I almost forgot what I was here for." The tips of his ears turned bright pink as he pulled a small notebook out of his shirt pocket. "And here I'm supposed to be this crackerjack reporter!"

"It's just because you're still new at this."

"Right." He cast a grateful look at her. Then suddenly his green eyes grew serious. "Okay, Chris, tell me. When did you first come up with the idea of doing a big research report on the history of Whittington?"

That was easy. Talking about the project was no problem, as long as Eric was listening and taking notes instead of asking a million questions about the town's history—one of which would be bound to make her slip up. Fortunately, he was content just to listen. She talked at great length about what she *did* know. And since Susan had done so much of the planning and given Chris so much guidance on how to research something like that, she had no problem sounding as if she knew as much about Whittington as her twin did. She even told Eric a few anecdotes about the town's history, little stories she remembered Chris telling her as she uncovered them in the course of her research. By the time their ice cream arrived, she was talking animatedly about Whittington—not only its history but also the way it was now.

Then suddenly, Eric's questions got tougher.

"Okay. I think we've covered that topic. Now some more personal stuff. First of all, tell me about your family. Do you have any sisters or brothers?"

Susan hesitated, pretending to be intent on stirring her milk shake with her straw. She couldn't very well lie, she knew; after all, whatever she said might be published in the newspaper. "I have a sister," she said slowly.

"Younger or older?"

"She's, um, older." That *was* the truth. Chris had been born seven minutes before Susan. Still, she was beginning to feel awful. She liked Eric too much to be holding back. Somehow, pretending to be Chris was a lot easier than having to answer a lot of tricky questions, questions whose answers ran the risk of exposing the Hot Fudge Sunday Affair.

What if I *do* tell Eric that I have a twin sister? Susan thought suddenly. He still won't know what we're up to. She wanted to tell him, but she was too afraid. As was usually the case with Susan, being cautious won over taking a risk.

Fortunately, the family background of the queen of Centennial Week didn't seem to be of too much interest to the *Herald* reporter. They quickly moved on to other topics: the classes she most enjoyed, her hobbies, what she wanted to do when she grew up. Susan answered the way she knew Chris would answer. And she downplayed her "interest in art" as much as she could. She was glad she knew her sister as well as she did. Pretending to be Chris was a breeze. If only that nagging feeling that she was deceiving Eric would go away . . .

"Well, I think I've got everything I need," Eric finally said, closing his notebook and tucking it back into his shirt pocket.

Instead of feeling relieved, Susan was disappointed. "I guess that means our interview is over, then."

"Not necessarily. I mean I don't have to hurry off or anything." Susan was pleased to see that Eric's ears turned pink again. It was becoming more and more obvious to her that he saw spending time with her as much more than just the tiresome duty of an up-and-coming reporter. She was determined to drink her milk shake as slowly as was humanly possible. In fact, she even wondered if she could possibly manage to down another.

"Good. In that case," she said, "let's try turning the tables."

"What do you mean?"

"Now it's *my* turn to interview you!" Susan's brown eyes glowed flirtatiously. "Let's see if I can find out what makes Eric Caulfield tick!"

Nine

Chris and her mother strolled up the sidewalk together, back toward the Pratts' house.

"That was some kitchen," Chris commented. "They've certainly put a lot of work into it. And I've never seen so many appliances in one place in my entire life. Except maybe at Sears."

Mrs. Pratt laughed. "You've got a good sense of humor, Chris. I'll bet you're doing a fine job as the queen of Centennial Week. Even though the selection was based on your research paper and the mayor had never even met you before this week, they couldn't have chosen someone more personable. More outgoing. Why, I can't think of anyone who'd be as good a representative of Whittington's young people as you."

"Oh, I don't know. Anyone could do it, I think. It's not really that hard . . . and it's an awful lot of fun." Chris was relieved that she and her mother had reached the back door at that point. She hoped her parents never noticed that she and her twin started to grow uncomfortable every time the subject of Centennial Week was raised.

"Perhaps," her mother was saying. "At any rate, I want you to know how proud your father and I are of you. And I'm sure that Susan's proud of you, too."

Chris gulped and dashed inside the kitchen, muttering, "Thanks, Mom." She hoped it appeared that her peculiar reaction was simply a matter of modesty. She felt more strongly than ever that it was time for her and her twin to have a heart-to-heart talk. The Hot Fudge Sunday Affair was threatening to get out of hand, and it was definitely time for a reevaluation. Still, she wasn't sure if she wanted Susan to agree to abandon it . . . or talk her into continuing. She intended to talk to her the very first chance she got.

As she went inside the house, she jumped. There, sitting at the kitchen table calmly drinking a glass of milk, was the last person in the world she would have expected to find: Jeff Miller.

"Jeff!" she gasped. She grabbed on to the refrigerator handle for support, suddenly feeling weak in the knees. "What are *you* doing here?"

"Hi!" he said cheerfully, wiping off his milk mustache. "Surprised, huh? I thought you would be." Gesturing toward his nearly empty glass, he added, "Your father offered me a glass of milk, so I said I'd just come on into the kitchen and help myself. You don't mind, do you?"

"Not at all. Help yourself, Jeff!" Mrs. Pratt had come into the kitchen behind Chris. "I'm Chris's mother. And I'm very pleased to meet the king of

Centennial Week. I must say we've already heard a lot about you."

Anxious to keep their conversation to a minimum, Chris interrupted immediately. "Hey, listen, Jeff. I just had a great idea. I've suddenly got this incredible urge for a chocolate ice cream soda. What do you say you and I hop on over to Fozzy's?"

"Yes, that sounds like fun. Have a nice time, kids." With that, Mrs. Pratt walked out of the kitchen. It was all Chris could do to suppress a loud sigh of relief.

"So I guess you really were surprised to see me," Jeff said as he and Chris sauntered past the dry cleaner's and the florist, toward Fozzy's. "Frankly, I wouldn't have been surprised if you ordered me out of your house the instant you laid eyes on me."

"I'd never do something like that!"

"I know. But I kind of feel like that's exactly what I deserved." He kept his eyes on the sidewalk. "Listen, Chris, I owe you a big apology. I acted like a real jerk yesterday. And I wasn't exactly Prince Charming all day today, either. I guess I overreacted."

He looked over at her then, and the expression in his eyes was apologetic. She noticed for the first time that they were a wonderful shade of blue-green. "Do you think that being a queen and all, you might be able to find it in your heart to forgive me?"

Chris couldn't help bursting out laughing. "Of course I forgive you, Jeff. And I'm really glad you decided that you and I should be friends again."

As they walked the rest of the way to Fozzy's, Chris noticed that it was a beautiful summer evening, the kind that always made her feel restless—and totally unable to stay indoors. Going out for an ice cream soda, especially with someone like Jeff Miller, was the perfect thing to be doing.

And when Jeff reached over and shyly took her hand, she was certain that she had never felt happier.

Their romantic reverie ended abruptly, however. As soon as they walked into Fozzy's, Chris spotted Susan. She was sitting at a corner table with Eric Caulfield, happily chattering away over a vanilla milk shake. Chris involuntarily let out a squeal.

"What is it, Chris? You look as if you've just seen a ghost!"

If he only knew! she thought ruefully.

With that special sense the twins had about each other, something they could never explain, Susan also had a feeling that she and her twin were in each other's presence. She glanced over toward the door and saw her sister standing there with Jeff. And then she realized what it all meant. A look of horror crossed Susan's face.

But it was too late. Before Chris could think of an excuse to leave immediately, before she even had a chance to drag Jeff out of there bodily, he said, "Hey, look, Chris! There's a girl who looks just like you! Do you know her?"

And Eric, noticing the peculiar expression on Susan's face, had looked over at the doorway and spotted Chris and Jeff. "Am I seeing double?" he whispered, unable to keep his eyes off the phantom-like duplicate of his date for the evening.

"I guess I forgot to tell you," Chris said to Jeff. "I have a twin sister."

"That's incredible! I mean, I had no idea. Well, let's go over and say hello."

"No! I wouldn't do that if I were you."

"Why not? I'd like to meet your twin, Chris."

"Well . . ." She thought as hard as she could, trying to come up with an excuse. "Actually, she and I have kind of an . . . agreement. That we'll keep our lives totally separate. So if I run into her somewhere, I pretend I didn't even see her. And she does the same thing."

"Oh. I see." But from the tone of his voice, Chris could tell he didn't see at all. "Gee, I wonder how she knows Eric Caulfield."

"Oh, I introduced them." That was true, in a way. If Chris hadn't suggested that Susan take turns being queen of Centennial Week, she never would have met him. "And, um, I think you'd better not say anything to him about it."

"Why not?"

"Oh, I don't know." Again Chris's head was spinning. "I just happen to know that he's . . . *shy* about that kind of thing. He's the type of person who likes to keep his life as a reporter completely separate from his personal life."

"Oh. Okay." Jeff still seemed a bit confused, but Chris was pretty sure that she'd managed to sound convincing.

"So," she said brightly, "why don't we go sit over there?" She pointed to the opposite corner of Fozzy's, to a table as far away from Susan and Eric's as possible.

Meanwhile, Susan and Eric were having a

similar conversaton. "So how come you didn't tell me you had a twin?"

"I told you I had a sister." Susan tried to sound matter-of-fact.

"Yes, but you said she was older."

"She *is* older. She's seven minutes older." She laughed, but Eric remained serious. He didn't seem angry as much as hurt, she decided. And she suspected that his reasons for feeling that way had less to do with his relationship with her as a reporter than as a friend. Perhaps even as a boyfriend.

He was looking at her, his green eyes clouded, waiting for an explanation.

"I guess I was afraid that there'd be too much emphasis on the fact that the queen of Centennial Week had a twin if you knew. Instead of the town's history or the research project or the honor of being chosen. Besides, Susan is very shy. I think she'd hate getting any kind of publicity."

"She doesn't look that shy to me." He glanced over at Chris. Underneath the table, she and Jeff were holding hands.

"Not with boys. Or with anybody on a one-to-one basis. I'm talking about being in the spotlight. You understand that, don't you?"

"Well . . . I guess so," Eric drawled.

"Oh, good! I knew you would!"

"Hey, how comes she knows Jeff Miller?"

Susan shrugged. "You know how small towns are. Everybody knows everybody?"

"Yes, but *you* didn't know him until this week."

"Just one of those things." Susan flashed her biggest smile, then stood up abruptly. "Well, I'm stuffed," she said. "I could use a brisk walk. Let's go over to the park. I can show you some more of Whittington."

"Don't you want to introduce me to your twin?"

"Um, some other time. Susan and I had kind of an argument before. Right after dinner. We're not exactly on speaking terms at the moment."

Eric had barely finished his pistachio ice cream. But he, too, stood up, still looking wary.

He had a feeling there was something funny going on. Aside from whatever reporter's instincts he liked to think he possessed, he was really beginning to like this girl. And that gave him extra insights into her. Yes, there was something peculiar in the air, although he was at a loss as to what it could possibly be.

He decided it was nothing more than a strained relationship between two sisters who happened to be twins. Maybe there was something mysterious in their past, some feud in the family that had never been resolved . . . And it was quite possible that none of it was any of his business. Still, he vowed to keep his eyes and ears open. He didn't like feeling as if he were missing out on something.

For now, however, he was determined to enjoy the rest of that evening. The mysterious twin at his side was already more than just the subject of his upcoming feature article. And if things worked out the way he hoped they would, the rest of the summer was going to be a lot better than he'd expected.

Well, Eric, he thought with a grin, you've certainly come a long way from kindergarten graduations and dog shows!

Ten

"Well, what do you think, Sooz? Have we gone too far this time?"

It was late Wednesday evening. The twins were in Chris's room having a powwow. Chris was sprawled across her bed. Susan sat beside her in an old rocking chair that had been in the family for years and had only recently been appropriated by Chris for her bedroom.

"Boy, this was the longest, *craziest* evening of my entire life! I was already beginning to have doubts. But when I walked into Fozzy's and saw you sitting there with Eric Caulfield . . . I think you and I had better take a minute to sit back and see where we are, okay?"

"Sounds reasonable," Susan agreed.

"Okay. First of all, we're not even halfway through Centennial Week, right?"

"Well, you could look at it that way," Susan said amiably. "On the other hand, you could also say that we've already managed to get almost halfway through Centennial Week without anyone catching on."

Chris thought for a moment. "That's true. I suppose that it's all a question of how you look at it. On that point, anyway."

"Definitely." Susan nodded emphatically.

"Okay. Second of all, Jeff Miller, who happens to be a key player in this episode, is beginning to think that one Christine Pratt is totally off her rocker. If you'll excuse the expression. I mean when we were at Fozzy's tonight and I told him I wouldn't introduce him to my very own twin sister because of . . . of some stupid agreement we had, I thought he was going to burst out laughing!"

"But he didn't."

"No, he didn't. But still . . . I felt really weird making up a story like that."

"Maybe," Susan said calmly. "But the fact remains that Jeff bought it and that awkward, embarrassing moment passed."

"Well . . . yes."

"And how are things between you two now?"

Chris closed her eyes and smiled. A dreamy expression softened her whole face. "Couldn't be better. I'm pretty certain that this king and queen are going to be continuing their royal relationship long after the glory of Centennial Week has passed." She opened her eyes suddenly. "Unless, of course, something goes wrong."

"In other words, the Jeff Miller situation is more or less under control."

"More or less. Yes, I guess you could say that. But wait!" Chris went on, sitting upright. "What about Eric Caulfield?"

"What *about* Eric Caulfield?"

"Now *he* presents us with double trouble. First of all, there are the social aspects."

"Meaning?"

"That you two are—if I read the signals correctly—embarking on a little romance of your own."

Susan turned a pleasant shade of pink, and a small smile crept across her lips. "I'm not about to deny it."

"Ah-hah! There it is! Another complication!"

"Another *potential* complication." Susan was quick to correct her.

"All right. But that's only half of it. And the lesser half, I might add. We can't forget the fact that Eric Caulfield is a newspaper reporter. Sure he has his charm, and those big blue eyes of his . . ."

"They're green!"

"Blue, green, whatever. His job, my dear twin, is to tell the world about people who are doing things they shouldn't be doing!"

"Yes, that's true. But you're forgetting one important thing."

"What?" Chris blinked.

"First, he has to *find out* that people are doing things they should'nt be doing! And the whole idea of the Hot Fudge Sunday Affair is to keep that little fact a secret!"

"But he already knows we're twins! I mean he knows that Chris Pratt has a twin."

Susan still refused to become distraught. "Yes, he does know that. And as far as I can tell, that hasn't made him the least bit suspicious. Unless, of course," she added, wearing an expression of innocence, "you know something I don't know."

By this point, Chris was scowling. "Sooz, I get the definite feeling that you're unwilling to let me talk you out of us continuing with the Hot Fudge Sunday Affair."

"I'm just giving you the facts." Susan smiled at her sister sweetly. "You're entitled to draw your own conclusions."

"So what you're saying, then, is that I'm getting all upset over nothing. That even though we've already run into some difficulties—some pretty messy ones, too, I might add—we've both managed to work around them. And you're saying that there's no real reason to discontinue our plan."

"Exactly." Susan dragged herself out of the rocking chair and sat down beside her sister on the bed. "*You're* the one who's always talking about rising to meet the challenge and all that. Here's a challenge . . . so let's rise to it! We've come this far, and no one's the wiser. We've both been having a blast being queen, you've got Jeff, and I've got Eric . . . so why change anything?"

"I suppose." Chris pondered what her sister had just said. It all made sense; *everything* Susan said always seemed to make sense. But she still wasn't convinced. And she knew what was still bothering her. Jeff Miller.

"Sooz, what happens tomorrow? Here Jeff and I just had this lovely evening together"—the dreamy look came over her once again—"and tomorrow morning he's going to be faced with an entirely different person who's playing the part of his queen! What's going to happen then?"

For the first time since the beginning of their discussion, Susan, too, looked worried. "I guess you've got a point. In less than twelve hours, I'm

going to be faced with a lovesick football star who
mistakenly thinks I'm the object of his affections.
That could turn into a confusing situation, all
right."

"I'll say! I don't want everything to get all mixed
up again as far as Jeff and I are concerned."

"I don't blame you." Susan was lost in thought
for a minute. "And as far as I can tell, there's only
one way to handle it."

"What's that?" Chris was watching her twin
eagerly. By now she was convinced that Susan had
the whole thing in her complete control.

Susan shrugged. "We'll just have to tell Jeff
what we're doing, that's all."

"*What?* We can't do that, Sooz!"

"Why not?"

"Well, for one thing, one of our original agree-
ments was that we wouldn't tell a soul about the Hot
Fudge Sunday Affair."

"That was your idea, not mine. Remember? And
besides, I think you can see why that simply won't
work anymore."

"Yes, I guess you're right," Chris sighed.
Already she was trying to imagine how Jeff would
react to the news that he had been courting two
different queens all week. Still, he seemed to have a
good enough sense of humor that he'd be able to
laugh about it. He might even admire them for
being so daring.

"So it's settled, then," Susan concluded matter-
of-factly. "Tomorrow morning, first thing, I'll tell
Jeff what's been going on. Just think: Not only will
it end a lot of confusion and keep your social life

from being ruined. It'll also make the whole thing a lot easier. Jeff can actually *help* us."

"I hadn't thought of that, but you're right. He can give us the high sign when we're about to say the wrong thing and tell us the names of people we're supposed to have met already . . . things like that."

"See? This is all working out for the best after all. But I'll tell you something I'm beginning to realize." Susan was suddenly very serious.

"What?"

"We'd better make sure that Eric Caulfield doesn't find out! The more I think about it, the more nervous it makes me. And I'm not talking about my social life, either. I'm talking about the fact that not only are we trying to fool a whole town; we're trying to fool a reporter whose job it is to watch us constantly!" She shook her head. "Oh, I don't know, Chris. Maybe we *have* gone too far this time!"

Chris's response was a loud groan. She took a pillow and hurled it at her sister.

"Get out of here before we go right back where we started!" she exclaimed, barely able to stop laughing. "I thought we'd just sorted all this out!"

Susan headed for the door, squealing as she fended off the barrage of pillows that followed. "All right, all right! I'm going!"

"But seriously, Sooz, thanks for the pep talk. I really needed it."

"No sweat, Chris. After all, what are sisters for?"

"Especially *twin* sisters."

"Twins? Are we twins? Do you really think we

look alike? Maybe we could actually pass for each other. . . ."

Chris's response was another pillow, punctuated by Susan's giggles and squeals as she raced back to her own room.

Eleven

As she hurried inside City Hall on Thursday morning, Susan was actually looking forward to confiding her secret about the Hot Fudge Sunday Affair to Jeff. She felt relieved, in a way, as if something that was meant to be fun, but was threatening to become troublesome, was about to be put under control. At least that's what she *hoped* would happen.

Oh, dear, she thought, having momentary doubts. For all I know, Jeff Miller will expose us to the world.

But she didn't really think so—and neither did Chris. He seemed like a good sport. And besides, he wouldn't want to do anything to get Chris in trouble . . . would he?

There was a small crowd waiting in the mayor's office; Mayor Harris, Jeff, and Eric were already there, ready to go. Her little talk with Jeff would simply have to wait.

It was almost lunchtime when Susan got her first

opportunity to talk to him alone. After a busy morning, the group stopped for a luncheon given by a local cooking school. As a large crowd of the school's teachers and students mingled with their invited guests over delicious appetizers served by waiters carrying huge trays, Chris took Jeff aside.

"Jeff, I want to ask you something," she began casually. "How do you feel about practical jokes?"

"Practical jokes? You mean people playing tricks on other people in real-life situations? Like those old 'Candid Camera' reruns?"

"Something like that."

"Well . . . I guess it all depends on people's reasons for playing them. If it's just for fun or there's some good reason for it, I think they're great. As long as no one gets hurt, I mean." He looked at her quizzically. "Why? Are you about to tell me that somebody's playing a practical joke on me?"

"Not exactly. I was just curious about how you feel about things like that." She took a slow sip of the ginger ale she was holding. "Actually, I'm more than just curious."

Susan took a deep breath. Might as well just come out and *say* it, she decided. "Jeff, there's something important I want to tell you."

"What?"

She bit her lip and stared at her glass. "I'm not Chris."

"'You're not Chris.' I don't know what you're talking about."

"I'm Susan, Chris's twin sister."

Just as she'd expected, Jeff was flabbergasted. "What? You're . . . Who . . ."

She couldn't help giggling at his reaction. "Calm down, Jeff. People are beginning to look at you."

"Chris . . . I mean Susan . . . I mean *whoever* you are, will you please tell me what the heck you're talking about?"

"I'm glad you asked," she said calmly. She was actually beginning to enjoy this. "It's not really very complicated. You see, Chris—my twin—was chosen to be queen of Centennial Week because of the research report she wrote on the history of Whittington. But the fact of the matter is I put a lot of work into that report, too. Somehow Chris didn't think it was fair for her to get all the glory while I was left behind like Cinderella. So she came up with the idea of the two of us taking turns being queen."

"I don't believe this!" Jeff breathed.

Susan continued in the same matter-of-fact manner. "I had my doubts, too, at first. But actually it's not the first time we've switched places. That's another story, though. Anyway, we decided to give it a try. So on Monday and Wednesday, Chris showed up and played the role of queen. Tuesday it was my turn, and I'm back again today. Simple, huh?"

Jeff continued to frown for another minute as he pondered what he had just been told. Susan watched him expectantly, anxious to see his reaction. Suddenly he broke into a huge grin.

"Far out!" he exclaimed. "What a great idea!"

"I'm so relieved you see it that way!"

"And that certainly explains a lot. Boy, I thought I was really off the wall when I saw how differently you acted on Monday and Tuesday. And then there was that business about art. I take it you're the artist, not Chris. Yeah, I had the feeling something funny was going on. But I never would have guessed . . ."

"Good. That's the whole idea. You see, *no one* is supposed to guess. And so far," she couldn't resist adding, not without some smugness, "we've been doing such a good job that no one's onto us."

"Well, you did have a couple of close calls there," he teased. "So how come you decided to tell *me* about your little scheme?"

"Two reasons, really. One is that we figured you could help us carry this thing off. To be perfectly honest, you've been the most difficult person to fool. And the other reason is that well, you and Chris seem to be becoming involved. . . ."

"Yeah, yeah, I follow." Jeff seemed anxious to change the subject. "So tell me what you want me to do, Susan. I mean Chris."

"Rule number one." She laughed. "*Never* call me Susan. Whoever you're with all day is Chris, no matter what."

"Got it!"

"Aside from that, just be on the alert. If somebody asks me a sticky question or if I don't recognize someone I'm supposed to have met or if I forget myself and start talking about art class or something totally un-Chris-like, just jump in and bale me out. And remember: no one else is to know about this. *Especially* Eric Caulfield."

"You got it. Hey, let me make sure of one thing."

"Yes?"

"That *was* Chris I was with last night . . . right?"

"Absolutely." Smiling sweetly, Susan added, "Would we ever try to fool you?"

Just then Susan noticed that a girl about her age with long blond hair and a yellow dress that she recognized from the cover of a recent issue of a fashion magazine was heading in her direction. The girl was wearing a look of determination that instantly made her nervous.

"My goodness! Who on earth is *that*?"

"Felicia Harris. That's right; you two haven't met yet."

"Uh-oh. I've heard all about her."

"Just remember that Felicia and Chris met on Monday. You two are old friends by now."

"Hi, Felicia!" Susan said in as friendly a tone as she could manage. "It's nice to see you again."

Felicia smiled coldly. "How are you enjoying your reign, Christine? Is it everything you hoped it would be?"

"Oh, yes. It's lots of fun."

"And Chris here is doing a terrific job, if I do say so myself," Jeff interjected. He put his arm around Susan protectively.

"My, my. I see we're getting quite friendly," Felicia observed. "Which reminds me. Jeff, how would you like to be my escort for the big fund-raising ball Saturday night? It's the gala event of Centennial Week, you know." She tossed her head so that her long blond hair rippled around her shoulders.

"Thanks but no thanks. I've already got a date. And I'm afraid that one girl is all I can handle at the moment." Jeff grinned at Susan and winked.

"Yes, I suppose you do have your duty to

perform, being king of Centennial Week and all that." Felicia turned her attention back to Susan. "So, Chris, you and I haven't had much of a chance to talk, I'm afraid."

"Really? As I recall, you did quite a bit of talking on Monday."

Jeff gave Susan's shoulder a triumphant squeeze.

Felicia let her remark pass, however. "But I haven't had a chance to find out much about *you*! You're so quiet all the time!"

"Maybe she just hasn't had a chance to get a word in edgewise," a male voice said cheerfully. "Because there are so many people around, I mean. I find that Chris is most talkative once you get her alone." Eric Caulfield joined the other three.

"You two haven't met, have you?" said Jeff.

"No, not exactly." Felicia smiled at the memory of the scene she'd overheard between the reporter and Chris—or rather *Susan*, pretending to be Chris. "Let's just say I've heard about you. Chris here was just going to tell us all about herself. Weren't you, Chris?"

While Eric's first instinct was to defend Chris, he couldn't help being a bit curious himself. He remembered his sense the night before that there was something funny going on.

"One thing I'd like to know more about is the way you spend your free time," he said. "Besides painting, that is."

I never should have brought that up, Susan thought ruefully. And I'm sure Chris would be the first to agree with me!

Now she was faced with the problem of how much to say. As Susan, she could talk about art for hours. But what about tomorrow, when it was Chris's turn to take over again? Susan could feel herself growing flustered.

As if she were using radar, Felicia immediately picked up on Susan's discomfort. "Don't be shy, Queen Christine. Tell us all about your artistic abilities. I must say this is something I hadn't heard about before."

"She's kind of modest," said Jeff.

"But a queen *has* to talk about herself! The public wants to know these things." Turning to Eric, Felicia said, "And it's your job to make *sure* the public knows!"

"I'm sure Eric and Jeff have already heard enough about this. Why don't we go over and sit down? I think they're just about ready to start serving lunch. . . ."

"Yes, let's go," Jeff agreed heartily. "I don't know about you, but I'm starving."

When Eric began to move toward the tables as well, Felicia realized she was defeated. But that didn't mean she was ready to give up.

"Well, I just had a terrific idea," she said loudly enough for all three to hear. "I'm going to insist that my father invite Charles Applegate to the gala fund-raising ball Saturday night. You *do* know who he is, don't you, Chris?"

Susan gulped. She knew only too well.

"I don't," Eric said. He had already reached for his notebook.

"Why, he's none other than Whittington's own artist. Quite well known, too, I might add. I'm sure our queen here will find it most stimulating to discuss art, one of her greatest passions, with him. And I, for one, can't wait to watch."

"I don't think . . ."

"There you go again, Chris, being Little Miss Modest. I'm sure you two will get along just famously. As you will with Edna Partridge, the town historian. She'll certainly be at the ball. Now won't that make for a well-rounded evening? Queen Chris will have the chance to discuss her two specialties—local history *and* art—with experts in each field. I can't *wait* to witness this!"

With her chin held at an arrogant angle, Felicia turned on her heel and stalked away.

Eric was watching her carefully. Then, after a few seconds, he headed for a table. As soon as he sat down, he began to study his notebook, puzzling over the pages and pages of notes he had been taking for the past few days.

Jeff, meanwhile, stayed at Susan's side.

"Uh-oh. *Now* what?" he whispered. "I don't know how she managed it or why she's even bothering, but the mayor's daughter has just made it impossible for either of you two to play the part of queen on Saturday night!"

Susan just nodded. She knew only too well that that was exactly what had just happened. As for whether or not Felicia was on to their scheme, she had no idea. There certainly didn't seem to be any way she could think of that the mayor's daughter could have found out. But the fact remained that come Saturday night, Chris and Susan Pratt were being put to a sort of test.

And how they would ever manage to pass that test was something she simply could not imagine.

Twelve

"Hey, Chris, can I give you a ride home?"

It was late Thursday afternoon, and Susan-as-Chris was on her way into City Hall to telephone her father. It had been another long day, fun but exhausting, and while she had insisted upon wearing her *own* shoes this time, her feet were still sore.

When Eric spotted her on her way upstairs and offered her a ride, she was tempted to say yes. It would be so much easier than calling home and then waiting for someone to come pick her up.

Still, she remembered all too clearly the conclusion that she and her twin had come to the night before: "We'd better make sure that Eric Caulfield doesn't find out!"

"Thanks, Eric. But my parents won't mind picking me up. I'll just give them a call. . . ."

"Oh, come on. You live in the north part of town, right? I'm headed in that direction anyway. Besides, it'll give me a chance to see some more of Whittington. We'll make the Grand Tour. It seems to me that giving informal tours of Whittington is exactly the kind of thing the queen should be doing.''

Susan could feel her resistance weakening. Taking a drive with Eric did sound like the perfect way to end the day. . . .

''I might even be persuaded to drive by Fozzy's.'' Eric's green eyes twinkled merrily. ''I think a couple of ice cream cones might be just the thing for a hot July afternoon.''

''How can I possibly turn down an offer like that?'' Susan laughed. ''Let's go.''

Well, it will keep Mom and Dad from having to pick me up, she argued with her cautious nature as she followed Eric to his car. They've both had long hard days of their own, and I'm sure they'd appreciate it if I managed to get home on my own steam.

A few minutes later, Eric and Susan were driving down Main Street armed with double-dip ice cream cones.

''Ummm, this is good. I'm glad you talked me into pistachio,'' said Susan.

''I'll have to remember to include that in my feature article on you. The queen of Centennial Week, Christine Pratt, reports that her main hobby is painting, her best subject in school is history, and her favorite flavor of ice cream is pistachio. How does that sound?''

''Like the very things the citizens of Whittington are dying to know about their queen!'' Susan sighed and licked a particularly dangerous drip of ice cream off the side of the cone. ''Honestly, wouldn't you rather be writing about the new elementary school or the town library or something like that?"

Eric glanced over at her. He was wearing a puzzled expression. "You don't like talking about yourself very much, do you?"

"I guess I just feel kind of funny. . . ."

"Although *sometimes* you do. Maybe you're just moody."

"Well, I do have kind of a shy streak." Susan was growing uncomfortable. "Being in the public eye must bring it out in me."

For the rest of the ride, Eric and Susan talked about the layout of Whittington, the benefits of having your own car, and the mild summer they were having. But she couldn't forget the odd way he had looked at her. And the way he'd said, "Maybe you're just moody. . . ." She was beginning to get a funny feeling about Eric—and how much he knew.

But when he dropped her off in front of her house with a cheerful "Well, good-bye, Chris! See you tomorrow!" it was hard to believe he could possibly suspect anything. He didn't ask to come inside or insist on meeting her family or try to hang around as if he were sniffing out clues.

See? she thought. And here you thought the only reason he wanted to drive you home was so he could spy on you. You're starting to become totally paranoid, Susan Pratt!

She skipped into the house, feeling good about Eric. For the moment, even the challenge that Felicia Harris had set up for the twins for Saturday night, only two days away, was completely forgotten.

Eric, however, had not forgotten. As he drove

away from the Pratts' house, back toward Main
Street, where the *Herald* office was, he was deep in
thought. He still had a long evening ahead of him.
He hadn't started his feature article for Sunday's
paper yet. But it wasn't writing it that had him
concerned. It was deciding whether or not to tell the
readers of the *Herald* what the queen of Centennial
Week had been doing.

Or, more accurately, the queen of Centennial
Week *and* her twin sister.

That day, right before lunch, Eric had figured out
what was going on. The combination of Felicia's
odd behavior, Chris's nervousness, and his own
suspicions that something out of the ordinary was
going on had finally led him to put two and two
together.

Or one and one, he thought with a smile. But this
time instead of one plus one equaling two, one plus
one equaled . . . *one*!

They're certainly a clever pair, he thought not
without admiration as he drove through the maze of
residential streets. Switching off the way they've
been doing, fooling everyone. Everyone, including
the mayor. *And* me. And hundreds of other
people . . .

But not Felicia.

How had she ever figured out what was going
on? he wondered. Her reasons for wanting to
expose them were all too obvious. She was envi-
ous, perhaps because she'd wanted to be queen
herself, perhaps because she was simply a jealous
person by nature. But how did she know? Especially since she, like most of the other people

involved, hadn't even known Chris and Susan Pratt before this week.

Yes, she was a crafty one, all right. Somehow she had figured out what was going on. And Eric was anxious to know how. What her source was. Still, he wasn't too worried about that. He had a feeling that sooner or later, she would come to him, anxious to tell whatever she knew about the Pratt twins' scheme. After all, she was the kind of person who couldn't enjoy making trouble for someone unless as many people as possible found out about it.

Was that how he felt, too? he wondered as he pulled up in front of the *Herald* office. Was exposing the twins, telling the residents of their hometown exactly what had been going on, really so important?

The evening ahead was going to be even longer than he'd anticipated. Before he could proceed with his article, he had to do some hard thinking, make some decisions about where his loyalties really lay. He felt committed to his duties as a newspaper reporter. But he couldn't just ignore the fact that his growing affection for the charming Ms. Pratt was getting in the way. Even though he wasn't even sure which twin it was that he was so infatuated with!

But even as he sat down at the desk that had been assigned to him for the summer, there was something gnawing away at him. Yes, he cared about the Pratt twins. And he was open to admitting that he wasn't being totally objective in his coverage of this story. But the fact remained that this *was* his first big chance. He had been determined right from the start to show off what he could do with this article.

He was a newspaper reporter, and he had responsibilities. Serious, important responsibilities.

Like it or not, that was the way things were. With a heavy heart Eric put a piece of paper into his typewriter and began to write.

Thirteen

As Susan floated into the house, she was still lost in dreamy thought. She was replaying in her mind how pleasant it was driving around with Eric, enjoying the cool summer evening and devouring a luscious ice cream cone and feeling as if she didn't have a care in the world.

But as soon as she walked in, her twin jumped off the couch where she had been reading a magazine, and ran over to her.

"How'd it go today?" Chris asked anxiously.

All of a sudden the conversation that had taken place just before lunch came rushing back to her. And her good mood vanished just as quickly.

"I'm afraid we've got ourselves into a real jam!" wailed Susan. "One that's not going to be quite so easy for us to squirm our way out of."

"Is that Chris?" Mrs. Pratt came in from the study. "Hi, honey. How did it go today?"

Susan-as-Chris cast a rueful glance at her twin. "I was just telling, uh, Sooz here all about it. It was fun. You know, more of the same kind of thing. A few speeches, a nice lunch, a lot of running around to different places. I'll tell you and Dad all about it over dinner."

"I'm glad it's going so well."

"Actually, one particularly interesting thing did happen today," Susan couldn't resist adding, looking meaningfully at Chris. "I ran into Mayor Harris's daughter, Felicia, at a luncheon given by the Bonne Cuisine Cooking School."

"How nice! You met her on Monday, too, as I recall. She's just about your age, isn't she?"

"Yes, but she goes to a different school."

"A *boarding* school," Chris interjected. "One with horses."

"Is she nice?" Mrs. Pratt asked innocently.

"Oh, *very* nice. In fact, she told me she's making sure her father invites all kinds of people with different backgrounds to the big fund-raising ball this Saturday night so that I'll be sure to have the chance to meet them."

"How exciting! Who exactly will be there?"

"I know of two of the people." Susan paused for dramatic effect. "One is Edna Partridge, the local historian."

"That's wonderful! You two can talk about the history of Whittington! Maybe even fill each other in on some obscure details that the other doesn't know about."

"Terrific," breathed Chris. She was beginning to get nervous. "Who's the other one?"

"Charles Applegate."

Chris just looked blank.

And then her mother exclaimed, "Charles Applegate! He's Whittington's most famous resident! Susan, I can't believe that you, of all people, have never heard of him. He's a very well-known artist."

Chris gulped. "Oh," she said softly. "*That* Charles Applegate."

"Well, if you girls will excuse me, I've got a million things to do before dinner. Imagine, my little Chris, mingling with Charles Applegate and Edna Partridge! What a unique opportunity!" She hurried back into the study.

"Why don't we adjourn upstairs for a little talk, Sis?" Chris suggested, her voice controlled.

"Funny, I was just about to suggest the exact same thing."

Once the two of them were behind the closed doors of her bedroom, Chris let out a mournful yell.

"Oh, no! *Now* what are we going to do?"

She flopped onto the bed, mumbling, "We've really done it this time. And it's all my fault. If I hadn't come up with this stupid, impossible idea . . . I mean, one thing to try to fool our friends. But how did I ever believe we could manage to fool a whole *town*?"

"We *did* manage to fool the town," Susan said, rocking gently in the old rocking chair. "Everybody except for one person. Felicia Harris."

"Unfortunately, one person seems to be all it takes. Whether she knows about the Hot Fudge Sunday Affair or this is just some bizarre, horrible coincidence, the fact remains that on Saturday night, one of us is going to have to come up with some pretty tricky maneuvers." Chris buried her face in the pillow. "Oooh, Sooz, suddenly I feel like I'm drowning in hot fudge!"

Despite her anguish, Susan couldn't help laughing. And then Chris started to laugh, too. Before long, both girls were doubled over, shrieking with laughter and gasping for breath and holding their stomachs.

"Maybe it's not so terrible after all," said Susan once they'd both calmed down. "You know, we still have forty-eight hours until the fund-raising ball. All we have to do is decide which one of us is going to go, and then the other can spend every waking minute drilling her on whatever subject it is that she's not quite an expert on."

"That's true," Chris sighed. "Sort of like cramming for an exam." She thought for a minute. "Well, it seems to me that *you* should go. You know more about the history of Whittington than I do about art."

"Oh, Chris! That's not fair! To quote Felicia Harris, this fund-raising ball is 'the gala event of Centennial Week.' I'd hate to have you miss it! Don't forget, you *are* the real queen. I'm just the stand-in."

"Yes, but you're a stand-in who could easily spend an hour discussing the history of the town's fire department or the year the first Girl Scout troop was founded with Edna Partridge. I, on the other hand, would be hard-pressed to discuss impressionism and expressionism and I-don't-know-what-else-ism with Charles Applegate. Especially if Felicia were standing right there wearing that funny little smile of hers and waiting for me to make a fool of myself."

"Maybe you could pretend you have laryngitis. Then you'd have an excuse not to say anything all night. You could just dance with Jeff and eat all the wonderful gourmet food and have a terrific time."

Chris rolled her eyes toward the ceiling. "I think you've seen too many old movies on television, Sooz. If we're going to start doing things like that, we might as well pretend I've got amnesia."

"I know!" Susan chuckled. "You could say you have amnesia and that all you remember is that you're the queen!"

"I could make everybody bow in my presence!"

"And you could create royal decrees . . . like everybody has to eat an ice cream sundae every night or else go to the dungeon!"

"Here's one. How about if I banish Felicia Harris from my queendom?"

But Susan didn't appear to be listening.

"Chris," she said dreamily, "that might not be such a bad idea."

Chris bolted upright. "Which idea? Do you mean pretending I have amnesia or banishing Felicia beyond the Whittington town limits?"

"What? Oh, neither! I mean thinking of the crazy things people are always doing on television. In those old movies from the forties and fifties. Or even on the new shows."

"Uh-oh. I'm not so sure I like the way your mind is working, Sooz. I'm beginning to have visions of you and me dressing up like chairs or going to the ball in a helicopter or pretending we're the exterminators. . . ."

"No, no. Nothing that elaborate. This plan is a good, solid one. And the best part is I really think it'll work."

Chris shrugged. "At this point, I'm desperate. If

"Simple, yes. Obvious, sort of. But foolproof? I'm not so sure. . . ."

"We can't miss! What could possibly go wrong?"

"Well, it certainly sounds as if it'll work. Especially since no one suspects anything, so no one will be keeping an eye out for anything unusual."

"Except Felicia, of course."

"Except Felicia."

Suddenly Chris broke into a huge grin. "Come on, Sooz! We can fool old Felicia Harris! She thinks she can outsmart us, so let's show her that when two Pratts put their heads together, nothing can stop them!"

"That's the spirit! Hey, let's go to my room. I'll try on my dress, too. And I can see if I have any shoes that are similar to a pair you have. . . ."

"Great. I'll bring my jewelry box. We can compare our earring collections. . . ."

The two girls scrambled out of Chris's room, anxious to see if they could dress up to look exactly the same. They were both exhilarated by the new twist their scheme was taking. Suddenly, carrying Saturday night off successfully right before Felicia Harris's very eyes promised to be an exciting challenge.

Most important, the Hot Fudge Sunday Affair was still on, full speed ahead.

Fourteen

When Chris reported to Mayor Harris's office first thing on Friday morning, she wasn't surprised that Eric and Jeff were already there, ready to go. But she was surprised to see that Felicia had, once again, decided to put in a guest appearance.

"Why, *hello* there, Christine!" she cooed as soon as the honorary queen of Centennial Week walked in. "We meet again!"

"Hello again, Felicia. It seems that you're becoming one of the regulars around here." Chris and Jeff exchanged wary glances.

"Well, I like to go where I feel I'm needed." Felicia smoothed her dress, a simple black shift that looked as if it were made of real silk. It was very pretty, but definitely too dressy for a busy day of ribbon-cutting and handshaking.

"Are you planning to join us again today, Felicia?" Jeff asked nervously. "Play chaperone as we tour the city?"

"Not exactly. I've got plans for bigger and better

things today. I'm afraid you two will simply have to muddle along without me."

She turned to Eric, who was lounging on the couch, reading that morning's edition of the *Whittington Herald*. "Which brings me to the perfectly *marvelous* idea I had this morning, Eric. How about lunch?"

"I hate to disappoint you, Felicia," Eric said, sneaking a wink at Chris, "but you're not the first person to come up with that idea. People have been eating lunch for thousands of years. Maybe even millions of years, for all I know."

"Oh, Eric. You can be so clever sometimes. Too bad this isn't one of them. Would you like to have lunch with me or not?" Eyeing Chris, she added, "I think you'll find it worthwhile."

"Well, I really hate to miss the Cub Scout Jamboree, but what the heck. You know what they say about all work and no play. I'm all yours."

Despite his pretended reluctance, Eric couldn't help being curious. From what he knew of Felicia, having lunch with him was more than a way to simply eat or to pass a pleasant hour making conversation. No, she definitely had something up her sleeve. And he couldn't wait to find out if his suspicions about what it was turned out to be correct.

Chris, on the other hand, was less than enthusiastic about the social situation that was developing before her eyes. Knowing that Felicia had undoubtedly planned it all so that she would be a witness only made her even more nervous. Two entirely different concerns were plaguing her. One was that if the feeling that she and her twin had begun to have were correct, if Felicia really had figured out the Hot Fudge Sunday Affair, she could be planning to tell Eric all about it once the two of them were alone.

The other was of a different nature but almost as alarming. What if Felicia's interest in Eric *were* purely social? Would he be fickle enough to abandon his fledgling romance with Susan for a fling with the mayor's spoiled, self-centered daughter?

When it was time to leave for the big parade down Main Street being held that morning, in which she and Jeff were riding in an open car with Mayor Harris, Chris was actually reluctant to go. And when Felicia called after them, "Bye-bye, you two kids! Have fun!" and then added with a wink, "And Eric, I'll be seeing *you* later!" Jeff practically had to drag her out of the mayor's office physically.

"Come on, my queen," he said, anxious to help. "Don't let big bad Felicia get you down. Centennial Week is almost over already. There are only three more days left. Enjoy it! Just because she's decided to split a peanut butter sandwich with Eric Caulfield is no reason to have your day ruined!"

"I guess you're right."

"Besides," he added with much less enthusiasm, "at this point there's not much you can do. Just cross your fingers and hope for the best."

"Right again, I'm afraid."

Even so, Chris was determined to follow Jeff's first piece of advice. He was right. Centennial week *was* almost over. Sunday was the final day. Of course, Saturday night and the big fund-raising ball came first. . . .

But she decided not to let herself think about that now. Instead, she held her chin up high, stood up as straight as she could, and strode down the hall.

"Let's go, Jeff," she said, taking his arm. "We've got another big day ahead of us. Let's try to make it our best day so far!"

At Felicia's insistence, she and Eric went to Whittington's fanciest—and most expensive—restaurant. Chez Michelle was not too far from City Hall, and it generally catered to government employees out celebrating a promotion or someone's birthday. It was small and intimate, with pink linen tablecloths, soft music, and huge bouquets of fresh flowers everywhere. Eric had never been there before, and he was quite impressed. Until he looked at the menu and saw the prices.

"Not exactly McDonald's, is it?" he muttered.

"I assume the newspaper will pick up the tab," Felicia said matter-of-factly. "You do have an expense account, don't you?"

"Only for business-related activities," Eric replied nervously.

"Ah, but this *is* business-related." Felicia's cold blue eyes were gleaming. "I have something to tell you that I just know you're going to find *most* interesting. Trust me, Eric."

"Is this something about you?"

He was only teasing, but she took him seriously. "No. We can save that kind of thing for *after* Centennial Week, if you like. This is something that's related to your assignment for the *Herald*. You know, your big feature article on the king and queen, for Sunday's paper. By the way, how is that going?"

"Afraid I won't be done on time?"

This time Felicia had the presence of mind to be insulted. "I'm trying to do you a favor, Eric. I'm offering to help you. If you're not interested in hearing some inside information, of course . . . well, that's another matter entirely." With deliberate movements, she unfolded her pink linen napkin and arranged it in her lap. "I could always speak to your editor instead. He *is* a good friend of Daddy's. . . ."

Eric sighed. "All right, Felicia. You've made your point. Let's hear what you've got to say."

Felicia smiled slowly, her blue eyes glowing like a cat's. "I thought you'd come around to seeing things my way. But let's order first. I'm really quite hungry." She reached for her menu.

Eric made a face. Obviously she planned to draw out this dramatic performance of hers as long as she could. She was enjoying it too much not to.

It wasn't until she was halfway done with her chef's salad, more lettuce than Eric had ever before seen in one place, that she looked up and said, "Well, I simply can't wait a moment longer. I *have* to tell you what I've discovered."

"So soon?" Eric said dryly. But he sat back in his chair and listened.

Felicia pushed her salad away and folded her arms across the table. Her eyes narrowed as she said, "Eric, there are two Christine Pratts." She paused, waiting for the full impact of what she had just said to register.

So I was right, thought Eric. But instead of

giving Felicia any satisfaction by looking amazed or acting impressed by this inside information of hers, he made a point of remaining calm. "What exactly do you mean by two Christine Pratts?"

"Chris Pratt has a twin sister. Her name is Susan. They're *identical* twins," she added meaningfully.

"How interesting." By the tone of his voice, Eric made it clear that he found her little bit of information a disappointment.

"But wait! There's more! I haven't told you the really important part yet!"

"I'm counting the seconds."

"The two of them have been switching off, taking turns at being the queen of Centennial Week!"

"No!"

"Yes! From what I can tell, they've been switching off every day, although I'm not positive about the details. Still, I know for a fact that they've been doing it all along. Imagine, those two girls trying to fool everyone in town! What do they take us for, anyway?"

"And may I ask what makes you so certain about all this?"

Felicia leaned back in her chair, smiling triumphantly. "I listened in on a telephone conversation between the two of them. They talked openly about what they were doing, never suspecting that someone else was hearing every word."

So *that* was how she'd found out! And here he had been attributing her with all kinds of intuitive powers!

"So you actually heard Chris and—Susan, is it?—Susan admit that they were doing this."

"Absolutely! Besides," she added smugly, "I already had a feeling there was something funny going on."

"Really? How?"

"I just sensed that Chris Pratt was someone who couldn't be trusted."

I'll bet, thought Eric, turning back to his hamburger.

He polished off the rest of his lunch hurriedly, aware that it was getting late. If he wanted to join Chris and Jeff for the afternoon's activities, he had to get moving.

"So?" Felicia said impatiently.

"So what?"

"You're going to expose them, aren't you? In your article?"

"Definitely! As a matter of fact," Eric went on calmly, "I happened to come across something last night that will tie in with this discovery of yours quite nicely. An interesting . . . twist to all this. A historical fact about Whittington that's so obscure that I doubt even Chris Pratt herself uncovered it while she was doing her research."

"Historical fact? What are you talking about?"

"You'll find out."

"Oh, tell me, for heaven's sake!"

"Now, now, if I tell you everything, then you won't be surprised on Sunday. I have to leave you with *some* reason to read my article, right?"

Felicia frowned. She clearly didn't like being left out of things. But she could also tell that Eric was not about to budge.

"It seems only fair to exchange *my* piece of information for *your* piece of information, but I'm not going to push it. I'm simply not that kind of person." She pulled her salad back toward her and began picking at it.

Suddenly she smiled at Eric. But this was an entirely different kind of smile.

"Now that our business is out of the way," she said flirtatiously, "why don't we get down to more personal matters? You are going to the fund-raising ball tomorrow night, aren't you?"

"Of course. It's the last event of Centennial Week that I'll be able to write about, since my deadline is midnight."

"Then you'll be looking for someone to dance with."

Eric just looked at her blankly. "I never dance while I'm working. After all, I've got a job to do."

But Felicia remained undaunted. "Well, never mind. I'll have plenty to keep me occupied, with or without a dancing partner."

That devilish gleam had come back into her eyes. "After all," she said, almost to herself, "tomorrow night is going to be quite a night. *Quite* a night!"

Fifteen

There were four Christine Pratts standing in Susan's bedroom.

As Chris and Susan stood before the full-length mirror behind the door, even they were astonished.

"Look, Sooz!" Chris breathed. "I look like I've been cloned!"

"Or else *I've* been cloned."

They were both wearing the dresses their aunt Lillian had sent them from New York, delicate white cotton with full skirts, billowing sleeves, and soft ruffles at the necks. For the occasion, they had added powder-blue sashes around their waists, tied in front. Their shoes were simple pumps, not quite the same but close enough to pass anything but the closest scrutiny. They had even done their hair the same, each pulling it back on both sides with tortoiseshell barrettes.

Only jewelry had been a problem. The two girls had such different taste they could find nothing similar. Chris preferred big colorful earrings and bright bangle bracelets, while Susan tended toward more delicate pieces, like fine gold chains and tiny pearls. It was Susan who came up with the solution.

"All we have to do is remember to switch jewelry whenever we switch places."

"What if we forget?" Chris asked nervously.

Susan thought for a moment. "If anyone ever said anything, all we'd have to do is act like we'd lost it."

"I could see losing an earring," Chris returned after groaning loudly, "but losing two earrings, a bracelet, *and* a necklace?"

"To quote one of the famous sneaks of all times"—Susan grinned—"if anything goes wrong, just wing it!"

Now, as they stood in front of the mirror, just before it was time to leave for the fund-raising ball, even Chris had to admit that the jewelry, all of it Susan's, completed the outfit. After all, this was a rather formal occasion. The pearl earrings, simple gold bracelet, and heart-shaped locket all helped make the dress look even more special.

"We both look like queens," Chris said, looking at their double reflection.

"Yes, we do."

Suddenly Susan got very serious. "You know, Chris, this whole week has been kind of crazy. All this running around and trying so hard to act like each other, and your meeting Jeff and my meeting Eric . . . But there's something I want to say."

Chris looked at her twin, surprised by the earnestness of her tone. "What?"

"That I appreciate your coming up with this nutty idea just so I could share in the fun of being queen of Centennial Week. And putting up with all the problems it's caused so far. Even agreeing to go through with tonight. I just want you to know that, well, I think you're the best sister in the whole wide world!" Susan threw her arms around her sister.

After a few seconds Chris said, "Aw, come on, Sis. Don't be so mushy. You're going to wrinkle my dress." As she moved away, her sister saw that her face was flushed. "To tell you the truth, I'm really afraid my mascara will run. Besides," she added sheepishly, "you know I think you're tops, too. Don't think I don't know how lucky I am to have you for a twin!"

Susan gave her sister's hand one last squeeze. "Well, we'd better get going. Nervous?"

"Who, me? This is one of the greatest challenges of my career! I couldn't be more psyched!"

"Okay, then. Let's go!"

Chris had arranged to borrow the family car for the evening. While she was saying good-bye to her parents, Susan slipped into the backseat and crouched below the window.

"That was easy," Chris said as she drove out of the driveway, waving to her parents. "So far so good."

"My very first ride in a getaway car," came Susan's voice from the backseat. "Do I have to stay down here the whole ride?"

"It's safer that way. We don't want anyone to see us. Besides, it's only a few blocks. We'll be there before you know it."

"I hope so. I'm getting red marks on my knees. Hey, look! Here's that earring I lost a couple of months ago! Gee, I looked *everywhere* for it! See?

This is already turning out to have been a good idea."

As they drove into the driveway of Mayor Harris's house, Chris began to ooh and ahh.

"What? What is it, Chris? Oh, darn it! I'm missing everything!"

"Oh, it's so beautiful, Sooz! They've got tiny white lights strung over the backyard and paper lanterns in all colors . . . and there's even an orchestra over there! This is so exciting!"

"I want to see!"

"No! Stay down! There are lots of people around. You'll see it all soon enough!"

"Chris, if there are people around, how am I going to sneak into the house?"

"Oh, dear. I don't know. . . . Wait, I just had an idea. I'll go inside first. Wait five minutes or so and then just walk into the house, as if you were me. I'll be in the backyard somewhere."

"And if anyone notices me?"

"The cover story will be that I left something in the car and went back to get it. Try not to talk to anybody, but if you get stuck, just pretend you're me. I'll come up and find you the moment things get uncomfortable. Okay?"

"Okay. Hey, Chris?"

"Yes?"

"I have a feeling this is going to be a *long* evening!"

The first phase of their plan proceeded smoothly. Chris went inside, making certain to move away from the front door, into the backyard, as quickly as she could. She searched the crowd that had already gathered, looking for Jeff.

Shortly afterward, Susan walked inside with as much confidence as her twin and stole upstairs. She peeked behind each door on the long hallway at the top of the stairs. The first room looked as if it belonged to the mayor and his wife. The second appeared to be one of his daughters' bedrooms. Then she came across a sparsely decorated room that had to be a guest room. It seemed like a safe place to hide out. It even had a comfortable chair in one corner. It was far away enough from the door so that anyone peeking in would never even notice that someone was in the room. Yet it was close enough to the window so that she could see the festivities down below.

It all looked so wonderful! From the second floor the white lights looked magical, like strings of stars that had lowered themselves into the mayor's backyard so that they, too, could watch. The yard was already filled with people, all of them dressed to the hilt. Men in dark suits or white dinner jackets, women in fancy dresses, many of them floor-length, in every color of the rainbow. A huge dance floor had been built over by the pool, and the small orchestra played, their music floating up to the sky like balloons.

Susan watched, mesmerized. She couldn't wait to go down there, to be a part of all that! But for the moment, she would simply have to wait. She settled back in her chair, her eyes glued to the window as if it were a television screen.

Chris, meanwhile, was at least as appreciative of the elegance of this affair. She wandered around the backyard, admiring the beautiful clothes the guests were wearing, taking in the romantic surroundings, noticing uniformed waiters who bowed slighty as they distributed punch and champagne and tiny hors d'oeuvres. No matter how this evening turned out, she knew already that it was one she would remember for the rest of her life. How wonderful to be a part of all this, to belong in such a storybook setting. It was like a fantasy come true.

Jeff, too, looked impressed. As soon as he and Chris spotted each other, he came over.

"Some party, huh? Not bad for a small town like Whittington!"

"I've never seen anything like it. Oh, Jeff, I wish this evening could go on forever!" Then she remembered what still lay ahead. "Actually, it might end up feeling that way. Jeff, there's something I have to tell you."

"Uh-oh. Don't tell me you're not really Chris. Again."

"No, I'm Chris. But I won't be for long. I'd better explain what we've got going this evening." She took him aside to make certain no one could hear.

It was while she was filling Jeff in that Felicia Harris spotted them. She immediately came rushing over, looking as if she had been waiting for their arrival all evening.

"*There* you are! Our guests of honor! Well, *two* of them, anyway. Tonight this party is *packed* with guests of honor." She was wearing her hair up, an elaborate maze of French braids fastened around her head. In her lavender dress and high heels, which looked as if they were just a bit too high for her, Chris had to admit that she looked lovely. But this time knowing that didn't make Chris feel any less pretty. Tonight she was too excited to let anything get in her way.

"Hi, Felicia. You look really great tonight."

"Why, thank you! You look rather . . . nice yourself. But enough idle chitchat! Charles Applegate just got here, and I'm dying for you two to meet!"

"Felicia, Chris and I just got here, too," said Jeff. "We haven't had a chance to grab a glass of punch yet!"

"You can eat later. Meeting and greeting is what tonight is all about. You've got to mingle, not act like little wallflowers. Come, he's right over here. I'll introduce you."

Jeff looked at Chris questioningly. He knew that the town's resident artist was the one person she wanted to avoid. But she looked quite calm.

"That's so sweet of you, Felicia. But first let me just run upstairs and comb my hair. I don't want to meet Charles Applegate with messy hair. I'm sure it needs fixing . . . right?"

Felicia scrutinized her hair coolly. Although it looked fine, she couldn't resist saying, "Yes, you're right. You'd better fix yourself up a bit before you start mingling."

"Be right back!" Chris slipped back into the house quickly. That had been easy enough! Now, if things would only continue just as smoothly for the rest of the evening . . .

"Sooz? Sooz?" Chris poked her head into every doorway on the second floor, whispering her sister's name. Fortunately, it wasn't long before she found her, lounging in a big overstuffed chair, gazing dreamily out the window.

"Chris! Is that you? So soon?"

"It's your turn to go downstairs. Felicia cornered me first thing. Charles Applegate just got here, and she's just about to introduce us. I told her I was going to fix my hair first."

"Okay. I'm ready. How do I look?"

"Great. Oh, and Jeff is there, waiting for you. I just told him about our plan for the evening. He took it rather well, actually."

"Great. Okay, then, here I go!"

"Sooz!"

"What?"

"The jewelry! Don't forget the jewelry!"

"Oops. Good thing you're more alert than I am." Quickly Chris unfastened the bracelet, earrings, and locket. Just as quickly, Susan put them on.

"Now you're ready. Go get 'em, Sis!"

By the time Susan-as-Chris joined Jeff and Felicia, she was poised and relaxed. "Now I'm ready," she said, exchanging knowing looks with Jeff. "Lead me to Charles Applegate."

Once Felicia located the elderly man, standing apart from the rest of the crowd, she introduced them immediately.

"Charles Applegate, I'd like you to meet the honorary king and queen of Centennial Week, Jeff Miller and Christine Pratt. Chris here is a fledgling artist herself. She's been dying to meet you so that the two of you could talk about art together. It really is her passion. Here, why don't you both move over a bit so some of the others can listen in on your discussion? I'm sure it will be fascinating!"

"So you're interested in art, are you?" Charles

Applegate said jovially. "Do you paint, or are you just an appreciator?"

"Oh, no. I love to paint."

"What exactly do you paint, Chris?" Felicia asked loudly. Her tone captured the attention of several people standing nearby.

"Actually, I try to maintain a broad range. Everything from still lifes to portraits to landscapes. I hope to take a life class at the Adult Education Center next fall."

Felicia's jaw dropped open.

"What exactly is a life class?" Jeff asked casually. His eyes, however, were fixed on Felicia. He was enjoying her reaction immensely.

"It's a special kind of art class that concentrates on drawing live models. It's quite difficult but one of the very best ways of learning."

"I agree totally," chimed in Charles Applegate. "I've always been convinced that that was where I got my best training. What medium do you prefer, Chris?"

"Right now I'm doing a lot with watercolor. Gouache, especially. But I've tried my hand at oils, and I love acrylics. The colors are so brilliant! It's so much easier than mixing your own. And of course I've experimented with multimedia . . ."

Felicia was dumbfounded. And when she overheard two of the people who had been listening marveling over Chris Pratt's versatility and knowledge, Jeff thought she was going to burst.

"Gee, I guess Chris knows more about art than any of us ever suspected," he said with a triumphant grin.

Felicia was too busy fuming to answer. She

watched as Charles Applegate offered Chris some punch, then suggested they go off in search of some refreshments together.

"Tell me, what do you think of all those new styles?" he was asking as he led her away from the others. "The ones that are just being developed now?"

"Oh, you must mean the neo-expressionists."

"You just wait, Christine Pratt," Felicia said under her breath. "The evening has just begun. Especially for you!"

For the next hour or so, Susan had the time of her life. Once she and Charles Applegate had established their friendship, even making plans to get together again some time so they could talk more and even show each other their work, she was off on her own. With her king at her side, Queen Chris met dozens of new people. She chatted with them all, enjoying every minute, feeling perfectly comfortable. And then she danced under the colorful paper lanterns until her feet hurt. When Eric unexpectedly cut in on one of her dancing partners, she began to wonder if she was actually dreaming.

"Hi, there. How's it going so far?"

"Super! And all of a sudden, it's even better. When did you get here?"

"Just now. I'm afraid I got a bit bogged down in some last-minute research. For tomorrow's article. It's just about done, although I'll have to rush back to the office just before midnight to make sure everything's in order."

"Ah, yes. The article. I'd forgotten all about that." For the moment even that intruding thought couldn't spoil her evening. Instead, Susan relaxed and let Eric whirl her around the dance floor.

Just when things seemed to be totally perfect, she heard Felicia's voice once again.

"There you are, Chris! Why don't you and Eric sit this one out? I've got someone else I'd like you to meet!"

Susan gulped. She had a feeling that the woman standing at Felicia's side was none other than Edna Partridge, historian for the town of Whittington. It was time to make another switch.

She thought fast. Fortunately, the excitement of the evening had given her incredible presence of mind. "I'll be right there, Felicia!" she called gaily.

And then, a second later, she crumpled to the ground with a loud "Ouch! My ankle!"

Instantly a crowd gathered around her, gasping and murmuring, "What happened? Are you all right?"

Eric, his face twisted with concern, helped her stand up. "You okay? Did I step on your feet?"

"No, no. My ankle just gave way all of a sudden. I'm fine, really." She pretended to hobble around, testing it. "It's all right. If I could just put something cold on it for a minute . . ."

"I'll get some ice," Eric volunteered.

"Oh, no! I . . ."

"Here, let me help." Jeff suddenly appeared from out of nowhere. "That kind of thing happens to me all the time. Playing football, I mean. What you need is to take the weight off it. Come on, Chris. I'll help you upstairs. You can lie down for a few minutes."

Gratefully Susan leaned on Jeff as he helped her toward the house, leaving behind a crowd of sympathetic onlookers.

"Good work!" he whispered.

"I never could have pulled it off without you!" she returned gleefully.

The two of them were so wrapped up in basking in their momentary triumph that they never noticed they were being followed.

"I'll just make sure she doesn't need anything," Felicia said offhandedly to no one in particular. And she went into the house after them.

But she stayed behind, ducking into a doorway on the second floor once she saw them opening into the guest room.

"Susan! What happened?" she heard a familiar voice gasp just before the door was closed.

So, Felicia thought, slipping away without a sound, they're at it again, are they? Well, this time they're not going to get away with it. I intend to make sure of that *personally*!

When Chris returned to the party, still on Jeff's arm, her limp had almost vanished. Felicia was disappointed that few people seemed to notice her miraculous recovery. And those who did were pleased that it had turned out to be nothing after all. But she quickly rounded up Edna Partridge once again, determined to pick up where they'd left off. Even though she now knew that her efforts to show up Chris Pratt in public were all in vain. Those twins had managed to outsmart her once again, and she had to figure out a different way to expose them.

Sure enough, Chris spent a pleasant, confident half hour discussing Whittington's history with the town historian. This time a much larger crowd gathered to listen—and to comment on how impressed they were with the queen of Centennial Week. Felicia watched the whole scene, furious. But her mind was working away. Finally she had an idea. A smile crept over her face slowly.

Yes, she thought, beginning to feel better already, there *is* a way to expose what the twins are doing. And they've unwittingly laid their own trap.

After Edna Partridge had drifted away, promising to invite Chris over to her house for more such stimulating discussions in the future, Felicia pounced on her once again.

"Chris, dinner is about to be served. But I wanted you to know that I've arranged to have you sit next to Charles Applegate. After all," she added sweetly, "you two seemed to get along so well."

"Thanks for letting me know, Felicia." Then Chris added quickly, "I mean, so I'll know where I'm supposed to sit."

Just as she had expected, Chris immediately made some excuse to the people around her and started toward the house. Felicia went to work quickly. She pushed through the crowd, her heart pounding, her mind racing. She had to find them all, in a hurry. Where had Edna Partridge gone? Ah, there she was. And there was Charles Applegate . . . and as luck would have it, he was talking to her father. Now if she could only find Eric . . .

"Sooz, it's just me." Chris slipped inside the guest room again.

"How did it go?" asked Susan, smoothing her hair and tugging at her dress. "I take it it's my turn again."

Chris nodded. "Felicia arranged for the queen to sit with Charles Applegate during dinner. So I guess you're the one who gets to eat all that lovely food."

"I'll try to slip some into my pocket. You can eat it later."

"Thanks for the thought. That's fine for biscuits or cookies, but why don't you finish off the mashed potatoes by yourself?"

"Well, I'm starved. And it'll be fun to talk to Charles again. He's such a nice man."

"Have fun, Sooz. Think of me during dessert."

Susan had just headed out the door when Chris suddenly shrieked, "Susan! The jewelry!" She came running out into the hallway, pulling off her bracelet and unfastening her earrings. She was so busy trying to take them off quickly that she wasn't quite looking where she was going, and she bumped into her sister, nearly knocking her over.

"Chris! Watch where you're . . ."

The two girls suddenly froze. Almost involuntarily their eyes drifted toward the top of the stairway.

Standing there watching in amazement was a small group of people. Mayor Harris was in front, as if he were the leader of the little party. On one side was Edna Partridge; on the other, Charles Applegate. Eric was there, too, watching from over the mayor's shoulder, a look of horror on his face.

And behind them all was Felicia, smiling so smugly that she looked like the proverbial cat who's just swallowed the canary.

"Well, well, well," boomed Mayor Harris, thrusting his hands into his pockets. "I do believe I'm seeing double!"

Sixteen

The next few minutes seemed to last an eternity. Chris and Susan stood frozen, just staring at the group at the head of the stairs. When they finally looked at each other, their eyes were wide open. The expressions on their faces said exactly the same thing.

We've been caught!

And then, all of a sudden, the mayor burst out laughing.

"I guess I'm *not* seeing double!" he said. "If I'm not mistaken, I'd say there really *are* two of you! Well, I'll be!"

The twins looked back at him, unable to believe what was happening. Their fear turned to puzzlement. And when Edna and Charles and Eric all joined in with loud guffaws, they were totally astonished.

Felicia, too, was surprised by their reaction.

"What is everyone *laughing* about, for heaven's

sake? Don't you realize that there are *two* Christine Pratts?"

"That's quite obvious, I'd say," said Charles Applegate. "I can tell that even without my glasses."

His refusal to share her anger only made her even more frustrated. "But don't you see what they've been doing? Not just tonight, either. All week! These two girls have been taking turns being the queen of Centennial Week, and no one's even suspected what was going on! Except for me, of course," she added meekly.

But nobody was listening. They were still too busy laughing.

Finally Felicia stamped her foot and said loudly, "Will someone tell me what's so funny?"

Susan cleared her throat nervously, then spoke for the first time. "I'm with Felicia on this. I have no idea what's going on. Would somebody please tell me why everyone's laughing so hard?"

"It's like this," Eric began, stepping forward. "It's a little-known fact that . . ."

"Wait!" Mayor Harris interrupted. "Don't tell them. Not yet. We don't want to spoil their surprise. After all," he added with a wink, "these twins are obviously fond of surprises and practical jokes and things like that."

"Yes, I guess you're right." Eric grinned. "They'll just have to wait."

"Until *when*?" Chris and Susan asked in unison.

"Just until tomorrow," said Mayor Harris. "Then you'll find out everything. As for right now, we'd better get down to dinner. If I'm late, the caterer will have my head!"

The others started downstairs, still enjoying the joke, and the twins and Eric joined them. Felicia was not far behind.

"I don't think *I* should have to wait, Eric." She pouted. "After all, I'm the one who found out about their scheme. And I'm the one who exposed them. If I hadn't insisted that my father and the others come upstairs immediately . . ."

"Come on, Felicia," said Eric, slapping her on the back. "Be a good sport. For once in your life, why don't you try just rolling with the punches?"

He turned his back on her then, putting one arm around Susan and one around Chris. The burning glare she cast in his direction was wasted on him.

"Now may I have the honor of escorting you two queens down to dinner?"

Suddenly Chris's eyes narrowed suspiciously. "You don't seemed very surprised by all this, Eric."

"To be perfectly honest, I'm not."

"You mean you knew!" Susan cried. "Then it's going to be in your article! Have you been planning to expose us all along?"

"Relax. Trust me on this one. I guarantee that after tomorrow, everything will make perfect sense. And you two will be none the worse off for having it all come out."

"I don't know about that," Susan sighed.

"I think Eric's right," Chris said. "He seems like a guy who knows what he's doing. Why don't we just try to enjoy the rest of the evening and worry about the consequences tomorrow? Especially since he keeps insisting that there won't be any negative ones!"

Felicia chimed in. "Well, I, for one, have no idea why no one is in the least bit shocked by your attempt to fool everyone in the town of Whittington."

"Sorry to disappoint you, Felicia," Chris said dryly. "By the way, how did you ever figure out what we were doing?"

"I just happen to be a very sensitive, perceptive individual. . . ."

"Who has absolutely no qualms about listening in on other people's telephone calls." Eric was only too happy to finish her sentence for her.

"What telephone conversation? I don't remember. . . ." Susan thought hard, but her face remained blank.

"*I* know," said Chris. "It must have been on Tuesday, your first day as queen. You called to say you needed a ride home, and I answered the phone. We started talking about the Hot Fudge Sunday Affair. . . ."

"The *what*?" both Felicia and Eric exclaimed.

Susan blushed. "Oh, it's nothing. Just a little . . . code name Chris and I came up with. That's what we've been calling our plan to take turns being queen of Centennial Week."

Eric laughed. "Funny, I've been agonizing over a headline for my feature article all week. I think you girls finally helped me come up with something."

Jeff came rushing over then, his face flushed. "Chris! Susan! What are you both doing here *together*? I thought . . ."

"The jig is up," Felicia said sourly. "They've

been found out, thanks to me. And the worst part is no one cares!''

"Oh, we care, all right," Eric corrected her. "It's just that . . . well, you'll all find out tomorrow. Hey, we'd better sit down. I think the mayor is about to make a toast."

They quickly found their seats. An extra place had been set right next to Chris's, and Susan had a feeling it was meant for her. As she and her twin plopped into their chairs, they heard Mayor Harris say, "And Whittington had an extra treat. As you all know, we chose an honorary king and queen to preside over the Centennial Week festivities. But instead of just *one* queen, we've been lucky enough to have *two*! Stand up, girls. I'm proud to introduce Christine and Susan Pratt!"

Chris and Susan exchanged glances as they stood up amid a loud burst of applause and cheers. Once again they were thinking the exact same thing, feeling the same way. Although they still didn't understand the hows and whys, this evening was easily turning out to be the best one of their entire lives.

Seventeen

"What was your favorite part of last night?" Susan asked dreamily. "The lights? The music? The dancing? The colored lanterns?"

"I think my favorite part was when Mayor Harris discovered that there were two of us . . . and didn't blow a fuse!"

"Oh, Chris! You're getting so practical! Why, you're almost beginning to sound like me!"

It was late Sunday morning, and the two girls were strolling over to the park for the unveiling and dedication of Whittington's new monument. For the occasion Susan was wearing the new dress she liked so much, the pink-and-lavender one with the draped scarf at the neck. Chris wore the other new dress, the blue flowered sundress. They looked so different—so much like themselves—that people passing them on the street, also making their way toward the park, never even noticed that the two of them were identical twins.

"So how do you feel now that Centennial Week is almost over?" asked Susan.

"A little bit sad. After all, it was lots of fun, don't you think?"

"Oh, definitely. But," she added with a rueful grin, "I'm a bit relieved at the same time. Life is much more relaxing when all I have to worry about is being *me*. Spending half the time being *you* is not always so easy, you know!"

"So I understand!" Chris laughed. "But you don't have any regrets, do you?"

"Are you kidding? I still think the Hot Fudge Sunday Affair was one of the Pratt twins' crowning achievements!"

"Well, I can't wait to find out if Eric Caulfield agrees. Let's pick up a copy of the Sunday paper right after the ceremony."

"I'm afraid to look," Susan groaned.

"Relax. Eric said not to worry, remember? Besides," she added, her brown eyes twinkling, "you *do* happen to have an in with the *Herald*'s star reporter."

"I doubt that'll make much difference. But we'll find out soon enough. By the time the dedication is over and we're off to the big barbecue, we'll know how it all turns out."

The park was already crowded. Everyone in Whittington, it seemed, was anxious to see the new statue, then go to the picnic that was the final event of Centennial Week. Susan found a place in front, while Chris hurried up to the wooden platform that had been set up especially for the occasion. Next to it was a massive statue draped in white fabric.

Jeff was already there. His face lit up when he spotted her.

"Hey, Chris! I was beginning to wonder if you were going to show up! After last night, I was afraid you might chicken out!"

"Me? Never! One thing about us Pratts: once we start something, nothing can stop us from seeing it through." She sat down next to him. "By the way, have you seen this morning's *Herald* yet?"

"Nope. I decided to wait until after the ceremony. Then if it turns out badly, I can go drown my sorrows in hot dogs and root beer."

"What are you worried about? You're not the one who's been playing tricks on the residents of Whittington."

"Well, no, but . . . . Let's just say I've got a special interest in how the article portrays my queen."

When the mayor appeared on the platform, a hush instantly fell over the crowd. He nodded to Chris as well as Jeff and the handful of others who were seated near them. She couldn't be certain, but she thought the look he gave her was particularly meaningful.

"Ladies and gentlemen, good citizens of Whittington, I'd like to welcome you all to an event that is a fitting conclusion for Centennial Week: the unveiling and dedication of this new monument, which will grace our park from now on. Long after this week is over, this statue, which commemorates the founding of Whittington exactly one hundred years ago, will remind us of the spirit in which this town was built. . . ."

"I hope he doesn't talk all morning," Jeff

whispered. "I'm getting really curious about that article."

"Me, too," Chris whispered back. "Besides, Eric and the mayor kept saying that today, we'd all find out what everyone thought was so funny last night. I can't see. . . . Oh, look, they're going to unveil the statue!"

As the white cloth draped over the huge monument was pulled down in one fell swoop, the crowd gasped, then broke into spontaneous applause. Chris glanced over at it casually, then did a double take.

"Look, Jeff!" She stood up so she could get a better look. "That's a statue of *two* people, not one!"

Almost as if he had heard her, Mayor Harris said, "A lot of you will be surprised to see that the statue of Whittington's founder is actually a statue of two people. They were the Whittington brothers, George and William. Until very recently it was believed that George Whittington was the founder of our town. But recently our local historian, Edna Partridge"—he nodded in her direction—"discovered a little-known fact. Why don't you explain this fascinating piece of history, Ms. Partridge?"

"Two brothers!" Chris gasped. Slowly everything was starting to fall into place.

"Thank you, Mayor Harris. Yes, I recently learned, through my research, that there were indeed *two* founders of Whittington. The two brothers looked rather alike, in fact, and they used their similarities in physical appearance to help raise money for the town. They would both pretend to be George Whittington so that they could double their efforts for raising money for the town library and other important buildings. These two men, George and William, worked together to accomplish something they both considered worthwhile. And now, one hundred years later, I'm sure we're all appreciative of their ingenuity and spirit."

"Wow!" Chris exclaimed after the speeches were over and the crowd began moving slowly toward the picnic grounds. "So there were *two* George Whittingtons, just like there are two Chris Pratts! Oh, look, here's Susan."

The two girls hugged each other gleefully. "What a stroke of luck! To think that you and I were actually reliving history!"

"No wonder the mayor thought it was so hilarious when he found out you were twins," said Jeff.

"And Eric must have come across the true story of George and William on his own," Chris said, her brow furrowed. "I wonder how I managed to miss it in my research."

"Well, even Edna Partridge just found out, and she's the town historian!" Susan replied. "Hey, let's go get a copy of the *Herald*. Now that we finally know why everyone was so tickled that we were both pretending to be the same person, I can't wait to see what Eric wrote."

They found a candy store opposite the park.

"Ooh, I'm afraid to look," Susan said nervously. "*You* find it, Chris. Tell me what it says."

Chris had no trouble locating the article. There on the front page was a huge photograph of Chris and Jeff with Mayor Harris, a candid shot taken at the ribbon-cutting of the building site for the new elementary school. The headline read, CENTENNIAL

WEEK FESTIVITIES MADE EVEN SWEETER BY HOT
FUDGE SUNDAY.

"Oh, look, Sooz!" cried Chris. "You've got to
see this!"

Reluctantly, Susan peeked over her sister's shoulder. Chris began to read aloud.

" 'New meaning was given to the phrase "Whittington spirit" during last week's festivities celebrating the one-hundred-year anniversary of the
founding of our town. Amidst a whirlwind of
activities related to the town's history with special
emphasis on its present development, the honorary
queen of Centennial Week, a high school student
named Christine Pratt, exhibited the same kind of
ingenuity as Whittington's founder, George Whittington.

" 'George and his look-alike brother worked
together to double their productivity while raising
both money and enthusiasm for the establishment of
a new community. And Christine, with similar
pluckiness, has secretly been sharing the responsibilities and rewards of being honorary queen with
her identical twin sister, Susan.' "

"What a glowing report!" Jeff exclaimed after
Chris had read the entire article aloud. "He makes
it sound like you two are the most heroic citizens of
Whittington since George and William themselves!"

"And here we've been so worried," Susan
sighed.

"*You* were the one who was worried!" cried
Chris. "I had faith in the Hot Fudge Sunday Affair
all along."

"Christine Pratt! Do you mean to tell me . . ."

"Well, *almost* all along."

"Come on, you two. Let's head over to the picnic grounds. We don't want to miss out on the rest of Centennial Week."

"Besides, I'm anxious to find Eric." Susan's cheeks turned pink. "Well, I want to tell him how much I enjoyed his article!"

"Do you know who I want to find?"

"Who?" Susan and Jeff exchanged puzzled glances.

"Felicia Harris, that's who!" Chris exclaimed. "I can't wait to see the look on her face!"

Eighteen

The town park of Whittington, usually a quiet place, had taken on the atmosphere of a carnival. Throngs of people covered the huge lawn behind the playgound, strolling, playing ball or Frisbee, or just talking. Red-white-and-blue streamers cascaded from the trees, along with perky clusters of balloons in the same colors. Set up along the side were big tables laden with food, much of it homemade by the townspeople, from which enthusiastic volunteers doled out barbecued frankfurters and hamburgers and lemonade. The fire department band played energetically, rousing marches that had everyone humming or tapping their toes.

And presiding over it all just a few hundred feet away were George and William Whittington.

"I think they look proud to be a part of all this," Susan observed, glancing over at the monument as she helped herself to a generous dollop of potato salad. "Don't you?"

"I think they look kind of impish, actually," said

Chris. "Look at the expression on old George's face. He looks as if he's about to burst out laughing any minute. As if he's keeping the world's best secret!"

"That's something you girls should know all about!"

Susan and Chris turned around to see Eric standing there, a hot dog in each hand.

"Eric! There you are! We've been looking for you!"

"Should I be honored or scared?"

"Definitely honored," laughed Susan. "We just wanted to tell you how much we liked your article."

"Well, I should hope so! It was all about how clever Chris and Susan Pratt are. Who could possibly find fault with something like that?"

"That's true," Jeff said, joining them. "I noticed that the king of Centennial Week hardly got a mention, though!"

Eric slapped Jeff on the back. "Well, my boy, let's just say that these two here are an awfully hard act to follow."

"By the way," said Chris, "I've been meaning to ask you how you found out about Whittington's founders being two look-alike brothers. Somehow I never came across the true story behind George."

"Well, I could pull a Felicia Harris and tell you about what a thorough research job I did. But the truth is last Thursday evening, I simply picked up the phone and called Edna Partridge. I told her about the article I was writing and that I was looking for some kind of twist. That's when she told me about George and William and the little game they played."

"Speaking of Felicia," Jeff interjected, "look who just showed up looking like she's on her way to the country club."

It was true; today Felicia was decked out in crisp white shorts, a white shirt and matching sweater with bands of maroon and navy blue around the cuffs and collar, and white socks and sneakers. She looked as if she were about to say, "Tennis, anyone?"

"Hey, Felicia!" Eric called. "Come on over and split a can of root beer with your pals!"

She glanced over in their direction curiously. But as soon as she saw the four of them standing together, her expression changed to a frown. Still, she wasn't about to ignore them. Reluctantly, she sauntered over.

"Well, hello there. If it isn't the ghostly trio— plus the man of the hour himself. That was quite an article in this morning's paper, Eric."

"I was rather pleased with it, if I do say so myself. Of course," he added, putting an arm around each of the twins, "I did have a lot to work with. Imagine how boring that article would have been if all I had to write was 'On Wednesday the king and queen went here. On Thursday they went there.' No, the Hot Fudge Sunday Affair definitely added an extra punch to my reporting."

"I'm pleased everyone is so happy with how things turned out," Felicia said dryly. "Now, if you'll excuse me, I really have to be moving along. Being the mayor's daughter can be *so* demanding sometimes. But, well, you know how it is. Social responsibilities and all that." With that she flounced off.

"Good old Felicia," Eric sighed. "I have a feeling she's not going to change a bit for the rest of her life. But on to more important matters."

"Like who can eat the most hot dogs?" Susan teased.

"Hey, I happen to be a growing boy!"

"And *I* happen to be a growing girl!" Chris reached over for the coleslaw, piling some high on her plate.

"Better save some room for later," her twin reminded her. "Don't forget: You and I have a date!"

"Oh, I haven't forgotten. I'm just getting warmed up."

Eric and Jeff exchanged quizzical glances.

"What kind of date?" asked Jeff. "I thought maybe the four of us could go somewhere together after this picnic. For a drive or out to a movie . . ."

"It sounds good," Chris said, "but Sooz here and I have already made plans for later on." When the two boys looked crestfallen, she went on, "Come on, you guys! You seem to have forgotten what this week has been all about!"

"What do you mean?"

"Just that Chris and I have been planning our own little celebration to mark the end of Centennial Week. Of course," she added, "it was all based on the assumption that a celebration would be in order. And I think we deserve a pat on the back. What do you think, Chris?"

"Oh, definitely! You and I deserve a reward. But

even though this was supposed to be a *private* celebration, I think we can make an exception in this case. Agreed?"

"Agreed!"

"Pardon me, you two," Jeff interrupted, "but would you mind telling us what you're talking about?"

Chris and Susan burst out laughing.

"It's simple," said Chris. "Sooz and I are inviting you and Eric to join us at Fozzy's. . . ."

"We'd love to!" Eric broke in. "And I think I can even guess what's on the menu."

"Hot fudge sundaes!" all four cried in unison.

About the Author

Cynthia Blair first decided to become a writer when she was six years old, but it was twenty years before she realized that dream. She grew up on Long Island, earned her B.A. from Bryn Mawr College in Pennsylvania, and went on to get an M.S. in business from M.I.T. In fact, it was while she was supposed to be working on her thesis that she started her first novel. After four years of writing while working as a marketing manager for food companies, she abandoned the corporate life in order to concentrate full-time on her novels. She is the author of *The Banana Split Affair* and *Once There Was a Fat Girl* as well as several contemporary novels, *Battle Scars* and *Just Married* among thēm.

Ms. Blair lives in Manhattan with her husband, Richard, and her son, Jesse.

Teenagers Enjoying Romance, Adventure and Just Plain Fun...

JUNIPER  BOOKS